"If ever there was a critica
find a moral compass, it
an easy-to-read book tha

MW01690466

her to stay near to the heart of Jesus. While remaining biblically sound and truly relevant, Dan and Nicole tackle the tough issues of purity, morality, marriage, and relationships with love and compassion. If you know a young woman entering the most critical developmental years, this is a must-read!"

-**Mike MacIntosh,** *Founder & President, Horizon International Ministries*

"In a culture that promotes promiscuity and pleasure, girls are battling questions like "Why wait?" and "Is it worth the wait?" Nicole and Dan boldly answer these questions with biblical truth and practical insights. Their honesty, personal experience, and passion will encourage every reader looking for answers."

-Rob & Denise Salvato, *Calvary Chapel Vista, California*

"Finally, a resource that equips and encourages young women to wait until marriage! Dan and Nicole offer today's youth a fresh, honest, and biblical approach to the sexual issues they are facing. This is a must-read, as well as a great ministry tool for youth ministry leaders, pregnancy resource centers, and all those who mentor and counsel young women."

-**Margy Hill,** *Founder, Women's Ministry Connection, Vista, California*

waiting for The One

nicole leitz & dan leitz

Waiting for the One

Published by Agape Publishing, USA

First printing, 2007

Cover layout and design by Neil Godding.

Additional copies of this book may be purchased at waitingfortheone.com.

ISBN: 1-59751-998-7

Printed in the United States of America.

Acknowledgments

We, first and foremost, want to thank our Lord and Savior Jesus Christ. We don't know where we would be if it wasn't for His grace, love, and mercy. Ultimately, we wouldn't exist without Him. Thank You for blessing us with Your best.

We thank our parents for all their love and support throughout the years, for loving us even through the hard times and always standing behind our every decision. We love you so much!

Thank you Romy Godding, Cristin Novak, Cindy Barger, Wayne and Susan Caldwell, and Maryanne Hommel for the hours you spent editing and proofreading the manuscript of this book.

Special thanks to Sharon Fischer, Chris and Julie Warner, and Jason and Christy Duff for your wonderful insight, encouragement, and inspiration throughout the whole process of this book and throughout the time we have known each and every one of you. Also, to Charlie Campbell. This book would not have come together without your wisdom, encouragement, and guidance.

As you read this book, it is our desire that you see how amazing God's plan is and that you, dear friend, would sit at His feet and wait for His best!

Contents

Introduction

Over the years we have read numerous Christian books on dating, many of which were promoting some type of formula. A few authors even provided step-by-step instructions to find Mr. Right. Wouldn't that be nice? If only it worked that way. Unfortunately, "how to" procedures play right into the hand of our flesh. We tend to look for clear, concise information on how to find the right one *right now*. On the other hand, solid truth has proven there is no formula for dating or for finding *the one*. No checklist will help you find the man of your dreams. There are only four simple words to follow: wait on the Lord.

Our desire is to help encourage and teach you to wait on the Lord, and we pray this book will remind you of the grace, power, and love of our amazing God. Only He is worthy of our praise and worship. Only He is worthy of glory.

Before you dig in, know that God loves to lavishly bless His children. The key words here are *His children*. You must first have an intimate relationship with Him before you can fully receive His blessings. You must be one of His precious children to experience special, divine guidance. If you are, praise the Lord and read on. But if you are not or if your relationship is not very strong, we want to speak to you for a moment.

Where do you stand today? What is going on in your life right now? Do you feel so far down the wrong path there is no way to turn back? Are you trying, without much success, to fill a void in your heart? Have you accepted Christ, and then walked away? No matter how far you walk from Jesus, He is still behind you with

His arms open wide. He is waiting to give you a life beyond your dreams. He is waiting for you to accept Him. Jesus is the only One who can bear your sins, and cleansing only occurs when we choose to accept His sacrifice upon the cross.

The Bible records seven places where blood spilled from Jesus' body. Each time He bled, our sins were being forgiven. If you accept Him as your Savior, your sin is covered too.

1st place: John 19:1, *"So then Pilate took Jesus and scourged Him."* Jesus bled from His *back.*

Have you turned your back on the Lord, or walked away from Him to do your own thing? Is life about whatever you want, regardless of others' opinions or advice? Are you focused on sex, even if it is outside of marriage? Do you spend most of your time getting drunk, doing drugs, or becoming wealthy? Does life's meaning center around fulfilling these types of desires? These pursuits will end in destruction. The Lord bled from His back, knowing that you might one day turn your back on Him. He covered your sins; you are forgiven! Turn around; He will be standing right in front of you.

2nd place: John 19:2 records that *"the soldiers twisted a crown of thorns and put it on His head ..."* Jesus bled from His *head.*

What goes on in your mind? What do you usually think about? Do you fully desire to please the Lord, or are you preoccupied with a guy or girl you like—or don't like? Are your thoughts fixated on who might be talking about the party this coming weekend? Do you think about your parents and how much you love them? Or do you think about how unfair they are? What does your mind dwell on? The Lord bled from His head, knowing that someday you would have impure thoughts. He covered those sins; you are forgiven! Philippians 4:8 instructs, *"Finally, brethren, whatever things are true, whatever things are noble, whatever things are just, whatever things are pure, whatever things are lovely, whatever things are of good report, if there is any virtue and if there is anything that is praiseworthy—meditate on these things."*

3rd, 4th, 5th, and 6th place: John 19:17–18 reveals, *"He, bearing His cross, went out to a place called the Place of a Skull ... where they crucified Him."* When Jesus was crucified, soldiers drove nails through each one of His hands and each of His feet. Jesus hung upon the tree, waiting to die. Blood flowed from His *right hand*, from His *left hand*, His *right foot*, and His *left foot*.

Where have your hands been? Have you used them to hit a person? Have you stolen? Have you used your hands to tip alcohol, smoke a joint, or take illegal drugs? Jesus bled from both of His hands, knowing that someday you might use your hands against Him. He covered those sins. You are forgiven!

Where have your feet run? Have you walked away from the Lord? Have you run toward destruction? Maybe you have been caught in a situation you thought would never happen. Jesus bled from each one of His feet, knowing that someday you might run far away from Him. He covered those sins. You are forgiven!

7th place: John 19:34, *"But one of the soldiers pierced His side with a spear, and immediately blood and water came out."* Jesus bled from His *heart*.

Jeremiah 17:9, *"The heart is deceitful above all things, and desperately wicked."* Who has your heart? Are you holding onto it, looking for someone to give it to? Do you follow what your heart says? Our human hearts are wicked and naturally lead us toward destruction. Have you given your heart completely to a guy and now wish you hadn't? The Lord wants your heart. He wants you to give it to Him. Jesus bled from His heart, knowing that ours are deceitful and desperately wicked, knowing that someday we might give them to someone else.

In fact, Jesus literally died of a broken heart. Medical experts have determined that Jesus' beating heart actually burst. He died for every sin that you and I will ever commit. They are covered, and you are forgiven! If you think you have gone too deep and there is no way back, that could not be further from the truth. You can come back! You can repent of your sins because Jesus has already paid the price. He bled so you wouldn't have to.

Earlier we asked, "Where are you?" and we will ask again, where are you? Are you walking in God's light or do you feel surrounded by darkness? Is your soul thirsty, unable to be quenched? Are you hungry, but not finding satisfaction? Are you weary, burdened, and needing rest? Jesus is the Light of the World. John 8:12 encourages us, reminding us that *"Jesus spoke to them saying, 'I am the light of the world. He who follows Me shall not walk in darkness, but have the light of life.'"* You will not walk in darkness if you choose to follow the Lord's path.

Jesus is the living water! John 7:37–38 records, *"on the last day, that great day of the feast, Jesus stood and cried out, saying, 'If anyone thirsts, let him come to Me and drink. He who believes in Me, as the Scripture has said, out of his heart will flow rivers of living water.'"* You won't be thirsting for things that don't fulfill when you choose to follow the Lord.

Jesus is the Bread of Life! John 6:35 says, *"And Jesus said to them, 'I am the bread of life. He who comes to Me shall never hunger, and he who believes in Me shall never thirst.'"* You will never be spiritually empty or hungry if you choose to follow the Lord.

Jesus will give you rest! In Matthew 11:28–30 we find His encouragement: *"Come to Me all you who labor and are heavy laden, and I will give you rest. Take My yoke upon you and learn from Me, for I am gentle and lowly in heart, and you will find rest. For My yoke is easy and My burden is light."* You will find rest if you seek the Lord.

If you do not have a personal relationship with Jesus Christ and realize that a life committed to Him is what you are searching for, know that you can ask Jesus to be your personal Savior right now. Jesus desires to be the King of your life. Are you willing to ask Jesus into your life and allow Him to rule? If you are ready, then follow these steps:

1. Acknowledge that you are a sinner.
2. Believe that Jesus Christ died on the cross for you and rose again.
3. Surrender your life to Him and turn away from your sin.

You can pray something like this:

> *God, I confess that I am a sinner. I realize that I need Your forgiveness. I believe that You, Jesus, paid the price for my sins on the cross. I believe that You rose again from the dead and want a relationship with me. Thank You for saving me. Come into my life. Forgive me. Be my Lord, my God. I desire to turn away from my sins and begin to follow You. Change me and empower me with Your Holy Spirit to live my life for You. Amen.*

If you prayed that prayer, you are now a born-again Christian. Remember, you're not "religious." Instead, you have a personal relationship with Jesus Christ. Christianity is a relationship with the Creator of the universe, our Savior. You have been set free from the sin that destroys life. God has forgiven you. He has washed you clean and He no longer remembers your sins. He has promised, *"I will forgive their wickedness, and I will never again remember their sins"* (Hebrews 8:12 NLT). If anyone ever comes to you and asks if you're sure that you're going to heaven, you can say yes, because of what Jesus did on the cross!

Maybe you were raised in a Christian home but have walked away from Christ. You can start over, take a stand, and recommit your life to Him right now. We serve the God of second chances, and He wants to wash you clean and give you a fresh start. Choose right now to surrender to the Lord and walk with Him for the rest of your life. Pray this prayer:

> *Jesus, I have turned my back on You and I am sorry. I know that I am a sinner. Forgive me for my sins. Come and be the King of my life. I surrender my life to You and I choose to walk every day with You from this moment forth. Thank You for loving me and dying for me.*

If you have prayed either of these prayers, we would love to hear from you. You can e-mail us at danandnicole@waitingfortheone.com or you can write to us at P. O. Box 2562, Vista, CA 92085. We hope you are as blessed reading this book as we were in writing it.

chapter one

Waiting for God's Timing

For when God made a promise to Abraham, because He could swear by no one greater, He swore by Himself, saying, "Surely blessing I will bless you, and multiplying I will multiply you." And so, after he had patiently endured, he obtained the promise.

—Hebrews 6:13–15

Everyone has to wait. It is a big part of life. We wait for the red light to turn green, for the doctor to reveal our medical results, to hear if we were accepted into this or that college, or to know if we made the team. We wait to drive a car, to find out if we got the job, and even to receive the mail. All our lives we are waiting for something.

As Christians, we are waiting for the coming of the Lord, for our Savior to return and to take us to heaven. We are *"eagerly waiting for the revelation of our Lord Jesus Christ"* (1 Corinthians 1:7). More or less, we all know what it is like to wait. But very few know what it is like to wait like Abraham.

Abraham and his wife Sarah had no children. He was ninety-nine years old when God promised that he would be a father of many nations. God also sent angels with the message that Sarah would bear a child. Since Sarah was ninety years old, Abraham fell on his face and laughed (Genesis 17:17). What would your reaction be? I would laugh too. I can hardly picture being thirty years old, but ninety? Imagine being ninety years old and being told for the first time that you are going to have a son. That is crazy!

God had made a promise though, so whether Abraham believed it or not, it would happen. And it did eventually happen, but Abraham had to wait twenty-five years before God blessed Sarah with a child. I don't know about you, but I had a hard enough time waiting to get out of high school. Those four years seemed like an eternity, and they were not even a quarter of twenty-five years. Imagine having to *wait* for something for twenty-five long years!

Abraham and Sarah had no idea how long they would have to wait. They only held a promise. Maybe you are waiting too—for

God to reveal your future husband. Your whole wedding may be planned, except for the missing groom. You might be able to envision yourself gliding down the aisle to that special song. Perhaps your pretty little centerpieces are even chosen, but still you have no idea with whom you will share that exquisite day. Are you nearly out of your mind wondering who the guy will be? Unfortunately (or perhaps fortunately), the length of your wait remains undetermined. You don't know when you'll meet your future husband, how you'll meet him, or what he may look like. A week could pass or ten years could fly by before God chooses to unfold this chapter of your life.

Waiting for the one God has picked can be frustrating, but waiting truly reaps rewards. Experience teaches that the more one focuses on being single, the more difficult the waiting grows. To make this time more profitable, redirect your focus to God, and reflect upon these three encouraging reasons why God has us wait.

God Desires to Prepare You

Now may the God of peace—who brought up from the dead our Lord Jesus, the great Shepherd of the sheep, and ratified an eternal covenant with his blood—may he equip you with all you need for doing his will. May he produce in you, through the power of Jesus Christ, every good thing that is pleasing to him. All glory to him forever and ever! Amen.

—Hebrews 13:20–21 NLT

God is preparing you. Let's study this principle played out in the life of a teenager. Young David was a man after God's own heart. But since Israel was desperate for a king, they pleaded with God for Saul, who was very handsome and taller than most men. Regrettably, though, Saul didn't fear God. The Lord did want to bless His people with a great king, but Israel was too consumed with being like the surrounding nations, with having what they had, and having it immediately.

God instructed Samuel to anoint a king for Israel. The prophet had no idea where he was going or whom God had chosen, but he was willing to go. When God brought Samuel to the house of Jesse, he watched seven of his impressive sons pass by, not one of whom God had chosen. One was left: David. He spent most of his time tending sheep, but when his father called him in, God told Samuel, "This is the one." Although David was anointed that day to become Israel's king, he did not immediately take the throne. He was chosen to become the *future* king of Israel. For all David knew it might have been three years or thirty years before he became king. God used many years to train David, and if he hadn't grown, matured, and been prepared to become king, his reign would have been a disaster. In the process of waiting for God's best, envy and fear—envy of what others have and fear of looking different—can tempt us to become impatient. Israel didn't want to wait for a king; they didn't want to consider God's best. Interestingly, however, God would still bless them eventually.

God has given most of us a desire to be married. Some are called to a life of singleness, but if you are not, then God has created someone specifically for you. You may not know who he is or when the time will come, but you can be sure it will happen in God's timing; however, before marriage, you will go through a season of singleness, a season of waiting. Like David, this is your preparation period. We discover in 1 and 2 Samuel (read through these chapters if you haven't) that David endured many trials, kept his focus upon God, and matured immensely. David did become a great king, but he wouldn't have been one the moment he was first anointed.

God has singles wait as He prepares them for their spouses. I know how hard waiting can be, but keep focused on your Creator, and know that during this time God is carefully shaping you into a beautiful woman, one after His own heart. He is preparing you to fill your role as a wife someday.

Imagine walking to the starting line for a big race with no training or preparation. And no one would want to be in the front lines of battle and not know how to hold a weapon.

Imagine walking to the starting line for a big race with no training or preparation. And no one would want to be on the front lines of battle and not know how to hold a weapon. We want to be as prepared as possible. This goes for marriage too; preparation time is crucial.

It is interesting how many times my husband and I might have crossed paths before we actually met. I almost graduated high school one year early to attend Bible college. Had that happened I would have met Dan there, but I didn't. I also worked at a surf shop with many of his high school friends. Although he came in often, we never met there either. There were other situations like these when it wasn't God's timing for us to meet. God wasn't finished preparing me for Dan or Dan for me. We are convinced that if we had met any earlier we would not have been friends. He wasn't interested in girls like me and I wasn't interested in guys like him. Praise the Lord that we met in God's perfect timing.

God desires to prepare, mold, and shape you into the woman your future husband will be attracted to, into the woman who will fit your future husband's needs. Give your life to God and let Him work in you. What can you do to help during this time of preparation? First, read your Bible daily. *"Early will I seek You ..."* (Psalm 63:1). The more time you spend with Jesus, the more you become like Him. He changes you through His Word. Second, get involved in your church. Every church has so many needs. Just ask your pastor or someone in the front office. You could serve in the children's ministry, jr. high ministry, or helps ministry by cleaning or painting. Ask the Lord to show you your gifts and where to use them. Third, be in fellowship on a regular basis. Worship God for all He has done. This is the time we focus on Him instead of on ourselves. God used the time I spent reading His Word, worshipping Him, and serving Him to shape me into a woman fit for my husband. I needed a huge change in my life, and I am so thankful that God never gave up on me. Know that He will never give up on you either! Surrender this season of waiting to God and allow Him to work in you.

God Desires to Teach You to Stay on Your Knees

> *Therefore humble yourselves under the mighty hand of God, that He may exalt you in due time, casting all your care upon Him, for He cares for you.*
>
> —1 Peter 5:6–7

Let's get back to the story of Abraham and Sarah. Look at what Abraham did during his time of waiting. *"And so, after he had patiently endured, he obtained the promise"* (Hebrews 6:15). Abraham patiently endured his waiting season. During these times, God works in amazing ways. Notice, though, that nothing happened for Abraham until *after* he had patiently waited. Enduring can be so difficult, but God desires to teach you endurance and patience.

I believe the only way to endure any season is to remain on our knees. That does not mean literally remaining at home on your knees until a future husband walks through the front door. That probably won't happen. I am talking about being in a constant state of surrender, of giving your life to God and allowing Him to work instead of trying to work out your own life. For example, if you are interested in a guy, it is wise to constantly be surrendering the whole situation to God. You could pray something like, *God please take this if it is not of You, or work it out if it is You. I surrender to Your amazing plan and I only want Your best.*

It must have been so difficult for Abraham and Sarah to endure those twenty-five years. In Genesis, we see how hard it was for them to remain on their knees. Since nothing was happening in regards to Sarah becoming pregnant, she gave her maid to Abraham and instructed him to bear a child by this woman. Sarah supposed that since she was not having a baby any time soon, the promised son should come through Abraham and Sarah's maid. Abraham agreed and Ishmael was born; however, Ishmael was not the promised son. So many problems have arisen from those decisions, and these consequences still affect our world today. We learn from the Bible that Jews are the descendants of Isaac (the promised son) and Arabs are the descendants of Ishmael. To this day, there is continual warfare between these two nations.

The Bible says of Ishmael, *"His hand shall be against every man, and every man's hand against him"* (Genesis 16:12). If Abraham had knelt down before the Lord about Sarah's bright idea, none of that would have taken place. If Sarah had remained on her knees, she would have realized God didn't need her help. Waiting reminds us not to take matters into our own hands. We cannot fall when we are already on our knees.

As I mentioned earlier, waiting for a guy can be difficult. In junior high school, I became so boy crazy it was ridiculous. I was more boy crazy than all my friends, and the new guy I liked every week became my "project." I called him on the phone, sat next to him at lunch, and planned how to spend as much time with him as possible. Then at the right moment (usually two days later), I would tell him I liked him, and because I hated having to guess, would immediately ask him if he liked me (this is *not* the way to go). The worst part of my system was as soon as I had gained a boy's interest, the relationship would last no longer than three days, and then I was over it. Many innocent hearts were hurt during my junior high days.

Waiting reminds us not to take matters into our own hands.

Unfortunately, my strategies did not end in junior high, but continued through high school and into college. I didn't want God to work; I wanted everything to happen in my own way and in my own time. Then after my first year of college, I began to notice a guy I had known for a while. Although I had never liked him before, I began to constantly pray about him. Well, here is the kicker: this was the first guy who refused to become my "project," and the last guy I ever tried to manipulate. God used this situation, knowing nothing would happen, just so I could finally learn my lesson about trying to take matters into my own hands. If I had even begun to tell this boy I liked him, he would have been completely turned off. I learned it is not God's plan for a girl to search for her future husband, to strive to make it happen, or to be the pursuer. In fact, it should be the opposite. Girls, when you surrender and remain on your knees before God, He is going to work in a way that will be more amazing than you can imagine. Nothing happened with that guy, and I came out of the situation with a better understanding of true surrender. Later, when I met my husband, I was able to easily surrender so he could do all the pursuing. But that wouldn't have happened if I tried to take matters into my own hands. I let God work and simply remained on my knees.

Our perfect example of patient endurance on earth is Jesus. As Christians, we continue *"looking unto Jesus, the author and finisher of our faith, who for the joy that was set before Him endured the cross, despising the shame, and has sat down at the right hand of the throne of God"* (Hebrews 12:2). Three times the night before He went to the cross, He pleaded, *"Father, if it is Your will, take this cup away from Me; nevertheless not My will, but Yours, be done"* (Luke 22:42). Jesus committed His whole life into His Father's hands, He remained on His knees, and He endured the cross. Abraham entrusted his whole life into God's hands, he remained on his knees, and he endured through his season of waiting. After Abraham endured, he received the promise. After Jesus endured, He sat down at the right hand of the Father and atonement was finished. *"If we endure, we shall also reign with Him"* (2 Timothy 2:12). The Bible also teaches, *"For you have need of endurance, so that after you have done the will of God, you may receive the promise"* (Hebrews 10:36). During the gaps between a promise and its fulfillment, God will change you.

He has your best in mind, but He wants you to remain on your knees before Him. God desires that a woman wait for His perfect timing so she might receive the blessing, the promise, and a crown.

Perhaps you are thinking, "That's really powerful and encouraging stuff, but how am I supposed to apply that to my life? How am I supposed to endure?" I am so glad you asked; here is what I recommend to *help* you in your season of waiting: God has commanded us in His Word to make disciples, saying, *"Go therefore and make disciples of all the nations"* (Matthew 28:19). But in order to make disciples, you must first be discipled. Discipleship teaches us to be imitators of Christ and deepens our walks with Him. Discipleship instructs, encourages, and corrects. As a disciple, it is important to know and understand God's Word because *"all Scripture is inspired by God and is useful to teach us what is true and to make us realize what is wrong in our lives. It corrects us when we are wrong and teaches us to do what is right. God uses it to prepare and equip his people to do every good work"* (2 Timothy 3:16–17 NLT). When you go through seasons on your knees before the Lord, it helps to have someone encourage you. Find an older woman in your church to disciple you, pray with you, and instruct you. Make sure she is a woman who has a personal and growing relationship with the Lord. Also, find a woman that you trust, someone with whom you can talk openly. Go through a book of the Bible with her and ask her to pray for you and with you. Prayer is powerful, and through it God will strengthen and equip you for the season you are in.

God Desires that You Receive His Best

Now to Him who is able to do exceedingly abundantly

> *above all that we ask or think, according to the power that works in us.*
>
> —Ephesians 3:20

Often God's abundant blessings take time. While you wait, He is at work in your life, whether you believe it or not. I am sure I am married to God's best for me, but I had to patiently endure through a season of waiting. I needed to be prepared and perfected, and I needed to learn to constantly remain on my knees. God blessed me exceedingly abundantly above all I could ask or think. The man I am married to cherishes me, he loves me with an unconditional love, and he looks at me through Jesus' eyes. No other man would have ever treated me the way my husband does.

God has created one man specifically for you, and now that I am married to the one God made for me, I can't help but tell you that waiting for God's timing is the smartest decision you can make. I know what it is to like guys and have it not work out, but I am telling you that once you see the big picture, you will be so glad it didn't work out. I pray that you won't fall for the first guy who comes along and that you won't give in to the pressure of dating someone *you know* isn't the guy God has for you. Wait for God's perfect timing, whether you have to wait for two weeks or ten years.

When you fully grasp the reality of God's love, you cannot help but want to wait for God's best. Remember, Abraham received the fruit of the promise *after* he had endured. I held tight to this verse while I waited: *"But, beloved, do not forget this one thing, that with the Lord one day is as a thousand years, and a thousand years as one day. The Lord is not slack concerning His promise"* (2 Peter 3:8–9). God will work in His perfect timing.

He is never too late and He is never too early. I have found the more I prayed for His will, the more similar our schedules became. Soon I began to see that God's timing is perfect.

Claim His promises as your own, and instead of using your time of singleness to help God out by trying to find your future husband, let God teach you these valuable truths during your time of waiting. Remain on your knees while God is preparing you, and endure while He is working on your future husband. For after you have endured you will receive the blessing—God's very best.

chapter two

The Importance of a Pure Life

In everything we do, we show that we are true ministers of God ... we prove ourselves by our purity.

—2 Corinthians 6:4, 6 NLT

One of the most popular teenage talk topics is purity. It is constantly addressed because the world around us screams the complete opposite. If you desire to know how to walk in purity, you will not find the answers on the radio, on television, in magazines, at school, or in clothing trends. These teach us to ignore purity and pursue what feels good. The world declares, "If that is where your heart is leading, go for it." That advice couldn't be worse. Following your heart will lead you to an impure lifestyle. Why? *"The heart is deceitful above all things, and desperately wicked; who can know it?"* (Jeremiah 17:9). Purity is not a natural fruit of our flesh. The world has effectively corrupted the concept of purity, and many teenagers still fall into its trap. As for girls, popular society says that only the most undesirable ones stay pure. That is a lie, but unfortunately one that I bought into. God, on the other hand, asks every person, both guys and girls, to walk in purity, to be an example of purity, and to pursue purity. These tasks are not part of our human nature. We do not snap our fingers to suddenly become women of purity. Pursuing it is a lifelong task. In our pursuit over the next few chapters, we will consider the importance of purity, how to pursue it, and the power that lies behind a pure life.

Purity is an amazing character quality. It is not defined only by remaining a virgin until marriage. Purity is a lifestyle, surrounding and defining every part of a person. Although I am married, I still pursue purity. The greatest reason purity is important is because God's Word declares it to be. The Bible is filled with instructions on how to live in purity, love with a pure heart, and be an example of purity to others.

When I began writing, I did a little research on purity. The Internet sites for "purity" only brought up articles making fun of it. The dictionary defined purity as "the quality or state of being pure."[1] These were not very helpful. Finally, I turned to the Word of God. (I should have done that in the beginning.) Purity simply means being righteous in the sight of God; when He looks at you, He sees you as pure. However, we cannot be made righteous by our own strength or will. We are filthy and sinful. Righteousness for us can only come through the cleansing power and covering of Jesus' blood. God promises believers, *"Though your sins are like scarlet, I will make them as white as snow. Though they are red like crimson, I will make them as white as wool"* (Isaiah 1:18 NLT). Jesus' blood can make us pure; His cleansing makes us white as snow. It doesn't matter who you are or where you have been. The Bible explains that *"as by one man's disobedience many were made sinners, so also by one Man's obedience many will be made righteous"* (Romans 5:19). When Adam sinned against the Lord, we were all made sinners; but when Jesus went to the cross, His blood made us righteous and pure in His sight. Consider the following ways to exercise purity in our lives. Purity is applied to the believer's:

Purity simply means being righteous in the sight of God; when He looks at you, He sees you as pure.

… *Heart. "He who has clean hands and a pure heart … "* (Psalm 24:4).

… *Mind. "Beloved, I now write to you this second epistle (in both of which I stir up your pure minds by way of reminder)"* (2 Peter 3:1).

… *Conscience. "Holding the mystery of the faith with a pure conscience"* (1 Timothy 3:9).

… *Language.* *"For then I will restore to the peoples a pure language, that they all may call on the name of the* LORD, *To serve Him with one accord"* (Zephaniah 3:9).

… *Body.* *"Let us draw near with a true heart in full assurance of faith, having our hearts sprinkled from an evil conscience and our bodies washed with pure water"* (Hebrews 10:22).[2]

God calls us to have a pure heart, a pure mind, a pure conscience, pure language, and a pure body. In the book of Hebrews, we are instructed to wash with pure water. Let's consider purity under three headings:

Physical Purity

Physical purity is revealed by what a woman wears, in the way she presents herself, and how she speaks. The first two are what people initially notice—they are visible aspects of purity, part of an outward appearance—the third category reveals a woman's heart too, and it is observed in how she treats others. Again, being a virgin is not the only form of purity. Conduct and countenance count also. The Bible praises a chaste, virtuous woman, saying, *"Who can find a virtuous wife? For her worth is far above rubies"* (Proverbs 31:10). A pure woman is a rare find. How would you like to be a woman of great value, a woman whose worth is far above rubies? I long to be a woman of virtue. Chapter eight will present a more in-depth look at physical purity.

Mental Purity

Mental purity begins in the mind. Actually, that is where nearly everything starts. *"Everything is pure to those whose hearts are pure. But nothing is pure to those who are corrupt and unbelieving, because their minds and consciences are corrupted"* (Titus 1:15 NLT). What are you filling your mind with? Do you watch movies that you probably shouldn't or listen to graphic secular music? Are you constantly watching MTV and searching out magazines on the latest fashions? One of my employers allowed us to listen to any radio station we wanted, but standards have gotten so low, the words seemed like some sort of audio pornography. I got so sick of waking up the next morning with those awful songs stuck in my head. Somehow, I knew all the words, and if I heard even a hint of a song I could pretty well guess its message. Outside of work I always had worship music playing, but the interesting thing is only the secular music got stuck in my head. I didn't even own the kind of music that was playing in my head.

Consider how much more influential these messages are if you listen to them purposely. Thinking about one thing long enough will eventually lead the message to dwell in your heart. There are always the excuses, "I just listen to the beats or rhythms," or "There isn't anything else to watch on TV." Listen, there is so much good Christian music out there, and the industry is growing larger and faster. And when there is nothing good to watch on TV, turn it off and read a book. If you desire to live a life of purity, you really need to be cautious about what fills your mind. Being constantly on guard also includes asking the Lord to filter bad thoughts out of your mind. We all have undesirable thoughts or images suddenly enter our minds, but it is our job to ask the Lord to purify our minds and help us not to think or dwell on those things. A woman who desires her worth to be far more than rubies is a woman who pursues purity in her mind.

On the positive side, mental purity can be cultivated through daily Bible reading, prayer, and worship. These practices help keep our minds focused on God. So, try this week, month, or year to not fill your mind with MTV or secular music or anything else this world offers. Instead, go to your local Christian bookstore and pick up a new worship CD of whatever music style you like. Buy a Bible study that you can pop into your car stereo. Begin reading a new book in the Bible, and grab a journal and a pen to record verses that speak to you. Tape those verses on your car dashboard, bathroom mirror, or school folder. If you are visual, order a DVD series by your favorite pastor. Fill your mind with God's instructions. There are so many resources available for you at Christian bookstores, churches, and Web sites. The apostle Paul encouraged believers by reminding them, *"whatever things are pure ... meditate on these things"* (Philippians 4:8). I challenge you to begin cultivating a mind marked by purity.

Spiritual Purity

Spiritual purity is found in your heart, but is seen by the way you live it out. We are reminded that *"out of the abundance of the heart the mouth speaks"* (Matthew 12:34). Although people cannot actually see your heart, they can tell what it is like by what comes out of your mouth. What is filling your heart today? Is it anger, bitterness, jealousy, and hatred, or is your heart filled with love, kindness, and self-control? If you are filling your mind with horrible images or graphic music, and are actually allowing them to remain, those thoughts will dwell in your heart and soon be revealed by whatever comes

> *People get a glimpse of your heart by listening to what you say.*

out of your mouth. People get a glimpse of your heart by listening to what you say. Maintaining spiritual purity is the same as maintaining mental purity: through prayer, worship, and time in God's Word. What you fill your mind with is eventually what your heart will dwell upon. So when you take my challenge to fill your mind with godly things, your heart will be transformed and then good things will flow from your mouth. The more you grow in the Lord and the deeper your walk becomes, the more you will become like Him. He will transform your heart into one marked by purity and virtue. James reminds us to *"draw near to God and He will draw near to you"* (James 4:8). He will change your life, but first you need to draw near to Him.

You now know what purity is and how you can begin to walk in it, but just knowing the truth doesn't cut it. Having the head knowledge is only half the battle. You have to let that knowledge drop the 18 inches and reside in your heart. Don't miss purity by 18 inches! I put this verse in the Mental Purity section, but read it again and carefully note the next verse: *"Everything is pure to those whose hearts are pure. But nothing is pure to those who are corrupt and unbelieving, because their minds and consciences are corrupted.* ***Such people claim they know God, but they deny Him by the way they live. They are detestable and disobedient, worthless for doing anything good"*** (Titus 1:15–16 NLT, emphasis mine). You will prove you know God only by the way you live. Only knowing or just saying you know God amounts to nothing. You really need to know Him and then live for Him.

So, let me sum all this up. Purity is being righteous in the sight of God. Jesus' blood covers your sin and makes you righteous. When you give your life to the Lord, asking Him to forgive you for your sins, He will wash you clean and make you pure. Being pure isn't something that you can work for. You can't make yourself pure, God sees you as being pure when you have been covered and washed in Jesus' blood. You cultivate a life of purity first by what you fill your mind with (mental purity), then by making sure that those things reside in your heart (spiritual purity); and last, purity will be reflected in your speech, countenance, and conduct (physical purity). Purity is something we must constantly pursue. Even though I am married, I still pursue purity. Let's take a further look at how to do this.

chapter three

Pursuing Purity

Now set your heart and your soul to seek the Lord your God.

—1 Chronicles 22:19

How do we seek the Lord with our hearts? And how does it apply to purity? Consider these questions: What are you trying to accomplish? Is it your heart's desire to get married, or just to get that cute guy's attention? Perhaps you simply want to talk to him. Maybe your heart is set on winning the big game, making the team, or performing your best in a sport. When our hearts are set on an accomplishment, our lives automatically become devoted, and sometimes even consumed, with the challenge.

When I was young, my dad taught my sister, brother, and me to surf, skateboard, and snowboard. Surfing I liked, but was not great at it. A fear of big waves affected my ability. Skateboarding was also scary, especially after I smacked my head on the concrete. But snowboarding—there is no other sport like it! It became my passion. Even though I fell time and time again, broke bones, scratched my face, smacked my head, and bled, I was driven to keep going.

In high school, I set my heart on becoming a professional snowboarder. My life was devoted and I was consumed. I wanted it as a career more than anything, and I almost got my chance. The connections I needed were at my job—a skateboard and snowboard shop. All my paychecks were cashed to buy new boards, boots, goggles, pants, and all the other necessary accessories. Every year, my mounds of "old" equipment were replaced. I always needed each year's latest clothing and equipment, which of course included a giant trampoline. With my snowboard attached, I would practice my jumps even if I couldn't make it to the mountains. So I had all the right equipment, worked in the right place, rode with the right people (who were much better than me), and was willing to go all out for this. Yes, I was consumed. For a while snowboarding was all I would talk about, think about, or watch. Great guys from work took me snowboarding every week and taught me new tricks and techniques. I rode with surf shop managers, and met and rode with some professional snowboarders as well, improving immensely with their encouragement and coaching.

Snowboarding was exciting, and without even realizing it, I had put my walk with the Lord on the back burner. This is not how I wanted my devotional life to be, but there was no time left for the Lord. My drift away was not obvious. I did not wake up one morning and say, "Lord, You have been so good to me, but now I am going to put snowboarding first." No, I *gradually* began to compromise my beliefs. But through the Lord's leading, my obsession ended.

I never became a professional snowboarder, and I never even competed. Instead, I ended up moving to Hawaii (not a snowboarder's paradise), and quit snowboarding at the end of January 2003. I haven't snowboarded since—one of the best but hardest decisions of my life. The experience showed me how easy it is to become consumed with an idol. From it I have learned to ask myself questions. And it would be wise for you to do the same. How would you answer this question: What am I devoted to and why?

"Therefore be imitators of God as dear children" (Ephesians 5:1). True devotion leads us to imitation. In fact, imitation is one of the greatest forms of worship. For me, becoming a great snowboarder drove me to copy those around me who were better. I basically worshiped snowboarding by giving almost everything to be great at it. When our hearts are set on something or someone, we can easily become a worshiper of that goal. If you want to attract a guy, to get his attention, or even to get married, your thoughts, heart, and life will revolve around your desire until it

consumes you. We do not recognize it, but in the intense pursuit of our own desires, our thinking becomes distorted as well. Because my heart was set on becoming a professional snowboarder, I sacrificed relationships with my closest friends, and even though I heard it, I ignored the Holy Spirit's voice. Having our hearts selfishly set on our own goals can become a problem. We easily fall into compromising our morals and beliefs to get exactly what we want, and that is a dangerous place to be. I was consumed with snowboarding and it easily could have taken my life. That is what being an imitator of something other than God will do. I have seen it happen firsthand, not only in myself, but in others around me.

True devotion leads us to imitation. In fact, imitation is one of the greatest forms of worship.

When a friend of mine went snowboarding with one of his buddies, they found a sweet handmade jump located off the trail. Although it looked dangerous, they decided to try to do back flips off it anyway. My friend easily ignored the warning of his own common sense. When he did not land the jump, he moved away to watch his buddy give it a shot. His friend attempted a back flip from the jump, but fell, broke his neck, and became paralyzed. Although it does not always happen literally, our strongest desires can paralyze us. When our wills are not matched with God's, they stunt our spiritual growth and change our thinking, without us even realizing it. Red flags warn us of dangers in life, but a heart determined to get its own way foolishly ignores them. If I had not given up snowboarding when I did, I am convinced that God would have taken it away, and that would not have been pretty. I also can guarantee if I was still snowboarding, I would not be a

Christian. It was an idol, and the moment we allow idols into our lives, God in His love will destroy it before it destroys us.

To seek purity, seek the Lord. Become devoted and consumed with His presence. Make the Lord the center of your life, devoting every moment to Him and His ways. Being devoted to God is being devoted to purity, because He is pure. *"And everyone who has this hope in Him purifies himself, just as He is pure"* (1 John 3:3). Be devoted to reading every day, be in constant fellowship with Him, and live a life of worship. Put simply, be an imitator of the Lord. When you set your heart to seek the Lord, you will begin to talk like Him, act like Him, and shine like Him. You will become the fragrance of Christ, kindling a passion that will never need to be replaced. Instead of being given over to what you are seeking and then being destroyed, be given over to the Lord and inherit eternal life. When you seek the Lord with all your heart and soul, your desires will change into God's desires. His desires are much greater than what you will expect. His will for you is to walk in purity. The more you seek Him, the more you will desire and be given the power to live a pure life.

To be an imitator of Christ we must know Him and understand His character. Learn more about His life by reading the Gospels and by studying His life. Note how Jesus responds to comments, how He reacts to situations, and how He obeys every command. Desiring to know Him more and to be like Him is the beginning of being an imitator. "But," you might say, "Jesus is perfect. There is no way I could be like Him." If you are thinking that, then look at the life of Paul who declared, *"Imitate me, just as I also imitate Christ"* (1 Corinthians 11:1). Paul was in no way perfect, but he imitated Christ. You don't have to be perfect to imitate Christ, you just have to be willing. When you surrender to God and ask Him to make you more like Him, it is He who will shape you and mold you into His image. The Word tells us to *"imitate those who through faith and patience inherit the promises"* (Hebrews 6:12). Follow Christ's example and heed His Word and you may be surprised to find purity arising as a by-product of your quest to please Him.

God calls us to worship Him first, trusting that He will take care of our needs and deal with our desires, instructing us to *"seek first the kingdom of God and His righteousness, and all these things shall be added to you"* (Matthew 6:33). If you desire to get married, for example, set your heart to first seek the Lord. If you desire to win and be great at the sport you play, set your heart and your soul to first seek the Lord. If you desire to get that guy's attention, set your heart and your soul to first seek the Lord. If you desire to get that job, buy that car, or go to that school, set your heart and your soul to first seek the Lord! He will give you greater results than you could ever ask for. Be devoted to knowing Him and deepening your knowledge of His Word. Remember that you are made pure in the sight of God by His blood. Pursue purity and it will fill your mind, dwell in your heart, and be reflected in your conduct, speech, and countenance. Purity will reflect Jesus as your life becomes marked by it.

chapter four

Living in the Power of Purity

For his [Moses'] face shone with the glory of God, even though the brightness was already fading away. Shouldn't we expect far greater glory under the new way, now that the Holy Spirit is giving life?

—2 Corinthians 3:7–8 NLT

You are the light of the world. A city that is set on a hill cannot be hidden. Nor do they light a lamp and put it under a basket, but on a lampstand, and it gives light to all who are in the house. Let your light so shine before men, that they may see your good works and glorify your Father in heaven" (Matthew 5:14–16). Lights shine most brightly in darkness. If you have ever looked down from an airplane on a city at night, you will see thousands of tiny sparks. In the same way, Christians are called to be lights in this world.

A life marked by purity will stand out. People will notice and be drawn to you, desiring what you have. Consider how difficult, confusing, and even deceiving the dark can be. For example, would you rather walk through your home with all the lights turned off or turned on? I would want the lights on because I would be lost in the dark. So many lives are lost spiritually; people are walking in darkness. However, when you meet them they cannot help but see the difference in your light. The light of the Holy Spirit in you reflects of Christ's glory. In the Old Testament, we see God's glory literally shining from a human face when He met with His most humble servant on a mountaintop.

After Moses spoke face to face with God, his countenance was so bright that he wore a covering so no one would be blinded. When you realize God has made you pure by His blood and when you choose to cultivate a life of purity, your light will radiate more brightly than you could ever imagine. Actually, it is not your own light shining; it is God's glory flooding through you. We are given the promise that we *"shall receive power when the Holy Spirit has come upon* [us]*"* (Acts 1:8). There is power in a pure life and you can live in that power. But do not be fooled, this is not the kind of power most of the world desires. Man's usual definition of power includes fame, fortune, and riches. The power of the Holy Spirit is different because it gives life both here and for eternity. We can see a wonderful living example of the Holy Spirit's power in Peter.

Peter and his brother were the first men Jesus personally invited to be His disciples (Matthew 4:18). Peter had the amazing privilege of walking next to Jesus, learning from Him, and fellowshipping with Him daily. And of all Jesus' disciples, it seems Peter's temperament was one of the most extreme. However, he lived out miracles many others only hear about. This bold disciple stepped out on the water and walked toward Jesus (Matthew 14:29). Peter watched Jesus perform many miracles and was himself empowered to perform the supernatural (Matthew 10:5–10). Peter saw Jesus' face shine like the sun and he saw His clothes become as white as light (Matthew 17:2). But Peter also had his share of blunders—moments when he blurted out without thinking. One time, for example, Peter declared to Jesus, *"Even if I have to die with You, I will not deny You!"* (Matthew 26:35). He was certain nothing would cause him to deny Christ. And why shouldn't he be? Peter had witnessed Jesus' miraculous power firsthand, and Peter had walked on water. I mean, come on, if I was able to walk with Jesus the way Peter did, I would be saying the same thing.

However, not long after his great promise of loyalty to Christ, Peter in one evening repeatedly denied even knowing Him. The night that soldiers carried Jesus away, Peter was warming himself by a fire when a servant girl asked if he were one of Jesus' disciples. Peter angrily denied having anything to do with Him. At this part of the story I usually think, "I would not have denied Him. After all Jesus has carried me through, I will always declare that I know Him." But Peter was human and so am I. In our own strength, we can do nothing. I probably would have done the same as Peter, trying like him to fix things myself. The good news is we do not have to do things in our own strength any more! We have the Holy Spirit working in and through us. Look what happened to Peter when the Holy Spirit came upon him. In Acts 2 he was filled with the Holy Spirit, stood up, and preached the gospel, and that day three thousand people were saved. Look how God spoke through Peter and saved three thousand souls! That is the kind of power the Holy Spirit gives. When you let the Holy Spirit work in and through your life, you will be amazed at the power that fills you too.

"If you keep yourself pure, you will be a special utensil for honorable use. Your life will be clean, and you will be ready for the Master to use you for every good work" (2 Timothy 2:21 NLT). Your life will not be inadequate, meaningless, or ineffective when it is kept pure. When God has made your life pure through the covering of His blood, you are called to cultivate purity and be used as a vessel for God's honor. He will use your life to further His kingdom. God desires that everyone might have eternal life, and He has chosen to use you as His special tool. God will use you the way He used Peter, but first your life must be made pure. When you surrender to Christ and ask Him to cover your sins, He will make you pure, gently molding your life like a potter does the clay. Jeremiah shows a picture of that relationship: *"And the vessel that he made of clay was marred in the hand of the potter; so he made it again into another vessel, as it seemed good to the potter to make"* (Jeremiah 18:4). It is never too late, or too early, to place your life in the hands of God so He can make you into a vessel of honor.

When I was fifteen, my dad bought me a purity ring. Excited to receive such an exquisite gift, and to share my commitment to purity, I wore it on the finger a wedding ring would one day go. I wanted to present this ring, along with my virginity, to my future husband. People often asked what this ring marked by a key, a cross, and a heart meant. I explained that God had the key to my heart, and that He would someday give it to my future husband. As special as that ring is, wearing it does not make anyone pure. There are girls who wear a purity ring only when they are around certain people, but then remove it when it is not popular. Some have convinced themselves that simply owning and wearing a purity ring makes them pure, while others remove theirs altogether, hoping to feel less guilty by not having to look down at it.

Because purity is a decision to be made between a woman and the Lord, I would not try to persuade anyone to wear a purity ring. It is a symbol of a personal commitment to God, like a wedding ring. When a wife wears her wedding ring, others know she is committed to her husband. So too, when you wear a purity ring, you can use that to show people you are committed to God. When people wonder what you are wearing, it gives you an opportunity to tell them about God. Make sure, however, that your walk backs up your talk. You do not want to misrepresent Christ.

Living in purity, then, is different from obeying a code of moral behavior. Upholding a moral code may look good to others, but it is simply a choice of conduct. Behaving morally does not save anyone for eternity. Real power is Spirit-filled. Only the washing and covering of Jesus' blood can make us pure in God's sight. There is power in a pure life, and like a flawless diamond, a woman committed to purity is hard to find.

Diamonds are sorted into many different categories: size, cut, clarity, shape, carat weight, color, and more. The most interesting category to me is clarity. Diamonds come in different levels of clarity and are defined by inclusions. Most gemstones have some sort of flaws or impurities affecting their transparency and brilliance. A common gem falls in an *included* level, which means the diamond has many impurities. Diamonds in the *slightly included* level have fewer inclusions, but internal and external flaws can still be detected. After that, each level has fewer impurities until one reaches the very rare and costly flawless diamond level.

When it comes to purity, what level are you on? Have you given your heart and virginity away, and feel you can never be radiant again? Maybe you have only given your heart away or gone a little too far. If you have any impurities or imperfections in your life remember Jesus willingly receives us the way we are. We simply cannot achieve perfection in order to be accepted or used by God. That is why the Lord sent Jesus to suffer in our place. Only He could be the perfect, required sacrifice. If you are thankful for Jesus' saving grace, and desire to be radiant in His sight, offer your life to God. When you ask Him to cover you with His blood, He makes you a spotless jewel. Jesus can make you flawless in His sight.

> *If you have any impurities or imperfections in your life remember Jesus willingly receives us the way we are.*

Once we commit our lives to God, the pressure of this world grows stronger. At times, each day can seem tougher to fight temptations than the one before. It takes a lot to stand against the tide. It takes much strength to swim upstream. Thankfully, though, we do not have to stand against the world alone. We are promised that God *"gives us, along with you, the ability to stand firm for Christ. He has commissioned us and He identifies us as His own by placing the Holy Spirit in our hearts as the first installment that guarantees everything He has promised us"* (2

Corinthians 1:21–22 NLT). Remember that Christ has made us pure, and He calls us to cultivate that life of purity in our minds and hearts. Living purely is reflected in our speech, conduct, and countenance. Remember we must *pursue* purity in every season of life. It is possible, as we are empowered by the Holy Spirit. Through the shining testimony of that purity, He will further His kingdom.

chapter five

Truth about Sex

Or do you not know that your body is the temple of the Holy Spirit who is in you, whom you have from God, and you are not your own? For you were bought at a price; therefore glorify God in your body and in your spirit, which are God's.

—1 Corinthians 6:19–20

Ever since I was old enough to understand "things" I had always wondered how sex could be such a bad thing outside of marriage and then all of a sudden become so amazing after "I do." How could a few words change something so strictly forbidden into a wonderful blessing? My youth pastors and church leaders taught us that sex is bad so "don't talk about it, don't think about it, and above all else, don't do it until you are married." My parents, on the other hand, never talked about it at all. I was so embarrassed by the subject that when I heard anything about it my face turned red, my ears closed up, and I began choke. I did not know what to think, and since my parents did not say anything about it, I figured my youth pastors were right.

My public high school required we take sex education classes, but I was so upset and embarrassed that our teachers would present the topic so openly that, to be honest, I didn't learn much of anything. I sat through sex education, uncomfortable to be taught about such a sensitive topic with immature, eager-to-learn, high school students. The boys made jokes about the material we covered in class while I would nervously laugh, acting like I knew what was going on. The truth was I had no idea what they were talking about. I should have failed that part of the class.

To sum it up: my youth pastor said sex was bad, my parents did not say anything at all, and my school was passing out condoms. No wonder I was confused. Numerous other girls I have met felt the same. Unfortunately, when many of them marry, they are terrified because of their lack of knowledge. Other girls have shared with me a fear of getting married because of sex. I want to reveal the truth about this subject, and I hope this chapter will help you understand both its beauty within marriage and its consequences outside of marriage.

Truth: Sex, in and of itself, is not a bad thing! The Lord has created almost all of us with a sex drive (Matthew 19:11-12), but He also created a specific time and place for that drive to be fulfilled. The Lord created sex for marriage. Let's see what the Bible says about it:

"Now concerning the things whereof ye wrote unto me: It is good for a man not to touch a woman. Nevertheless, to avoid fornication, let every man have his own wife, and let every woman have her own husband" (1 Corinthians 7:1–2 KJV). Fornication is "consensual sexual intercourse between two persons not married to each other."[3] The Greek word for fornication is *porneia*, which means "harlotry (including adultery and incest)." The Bible commands us to avoid fornication. Understand that fornication is not limited to those who are married. Singles who are having sex are committing fornication. Paul teaches us on this issue in 1 Corinthians 7:8–9: *"So I say to those who are not married ... if they can't control themselves, they should go ahead and marry. It's better to marry than to burn with lust"* (NLT). The following few verses may help:

- *"For this is the will of God, even your sanctification, that ye should abstain from fornication"* (1 Thessalonians 4:3 KJV).
- *"God's will is for you to be holy, so stay away from all sexual sin"* (1 Thessalonians 4:3 NLT).
- *"Flee fornication. Every sin that a man doeth is without the body; but he that committeth fornication sinneth against his own body"* (1 Corinthians 6:18 KJV).
- *"Run from sexual sin! No other sin so clearly affects the body as this one does"* (1 Corinthians 6:18 NLT).

- *"Now the body is not for fornication, but for the Lord; and the Lord for the body"* (1 Corinthians 6:13 KJV).
- *"But you can't say that the body was made for sexual immorality. They were made for the Lord, and the Lord cares about our bodies"* (1 Corinthians 6:13 NLT).

When sex is enjoyed by a husband and his wife, it is not bad, scary, or shameful. God created it to be a blessing. He created sex for marriage. Consider the first couple God created.

> *And the LORD God said, "It is not good that man should be alone; I will make him a helper comparable to him." Then the rib which the LORD God had taken from the man He made into a woman, and He brought her to the man. And Adam said, "this is now bone of my bone and flesh of my flesh; she shall be called woman for she was taken out of man." Therefore a man shall leave his father and mother and be joined to his wife, and they shall become one flesh. And they were both naked, the man and his wife, and were not ashamed.*
>
> —Genesis 2:18, 22–25

The Lord created the man and the woman to be together in marriage. It is natural and perfectly normal to be attracted to the opposite sex. My hormones were exploding from junior high all the way until I met my husband, and I had little crushes on almost every boy I met along the way. Now, I am just crazy about one guy, my husband. The only downside to hormones is that it is extremely hard to keep them under control. When the body is maturing and changing, curiosity of the unknown grows stronger. In some cases, the more teens learn about sex, the greater their desire to experience it.

I attended public school through my sophomore year, but finished in a private Christian school. There was a huge difference between the two. Most of my friends in public high school had already had sex, and it was usually the topic of conversation. Because I did not know anything, I pretended like I knew what they were saying. Girls pressured me to "hurry up" and do it, and when they found out that I hadn't even kissed a boy, they went around asking which boys would be willing to be the first. I was so embarrassed and angry that I begged my parents to put me in a Christian school. I couldn't handle all their comments and jokes. It can be so hard to stay pure when almost everyone around you isn't.

You have God's promises to hold and the comfort of knowing the pressure will only last for a season. Sex will be wonderful in your marriage, not any time before.

In the Christian school I attended, other kids were committed to remaining virgins until marriage too. It was so amazing to not deal with the peer pressure. Instead of being torn down for my beliefs, I was encouraged by all my teachers to keep living what I believed. And to my great relief, I found many Christian friends were just as lost as I was about this subject of sex. I was not the only one. But maybe you do not have the luxury of going to a Christian school. Maybe you live day in and day out with pressure from unsaved friends. Be encouraged because *"No temptation has overtaken you except such as is common to man; but God is faithful, who will not allow you to be tempted beyond what you are able, but with the temptation will also make a way of escape, that you may be able to bear it"* (1 Corinthians

10:13). You have the Holy Spirit to help you resist giving in to those feelings or curiosities. You have God's promises to hold and the comfort of knowing the pressure will only last for a season. Sex will be wonderful in your marriage, not any time before. If you are tempted to just get it over with so your friends or boyfriend will quit pressuring you, think again. Giving in to the pressure is not the way to go. Try focusing on the future instead of your present situation. Instead of thinking about getting it over with, try to imagine the look on your future husband's face when you tell him you could not wait because your friends would not get off your back. Does that sound like a good reason to have sex? I don't think so either.

If you are not married, your body belongs to God. Consider how our Creator instructs us to care for it: *"Or do you not know that your body is the temple of the Holy Spirit who is in you, whom you have from God, and you are not your own? For you were bought at a price; therefore glorify God in your body and in your spirit, which are God's"* (1 Corinthians 6:19–20). God is asking you to glorify Him through your actions. Sex before marriage is not glorifying to God. On the other hand, once you are married, you still belong to God, but your body belongs to your husband as well. The Bible says, *"Let the husband render to his wife the affection due her, and likewise also the wife to her husband. The wife does not have authority over her own body, but the husband does. And likewise the husband does not have authority over his own body, but the wife does"* (1 Corinthians 7:3–4). In marriage, you will be his and he will be yours, and again there will be nothing to be ashamed of. This is how God created it.

All this said, you may still wonder, "If sex in and of itself is a good thing, why am I unable to understand how it goes from bad to good?" I asked many married women the same question. Read again Genesis 2:25, *"... and they were both naked, the man and his wife, and were not ashamed."* When sex is within the confines of marriage, there is nothing to be ashamed of. In marriage, sex is a beautiful physical expression of love. If you are terrified, don't be, because it will be amazing. The Lord knows your anxieties, your desires, and your fears, and He will always meet you where you are. The moment you enter into the covenant of marriage, He will meet you there, and sex will finally be good for you to enjoy. Understand that sex outside of marriage is forbidden, but within marriage it has His blessing.

Sex Is Awesome ... Unless Outside of Marriage

Sex outside of marriage will leave you feeling guilty, regretful, cheap, used, angry, stupid, ridiculous, embarrassed, and afraid of being pregnant. Girls become tortured by thoughts such as: *Is he going to leave me? Did he do this just to get what he wants? Why did I do this? Will God forgive me? What if I am pregnant?* If you think that having sex outside of marriage will be the most amazing thing ever, think again.

If you are thinking about having sex with your boyfriend right now, I pray that you would stop and really listen for just a moment. Here are the three biggest decisions you will ever need to make and why (in order of importance):

1. Your decision to accept the Lord Jesus Christ as your personal Savior, because eternal life is for real and your choice will determine your eternal destination.

2. Whom you choose to marry. Aside from what the

world says, this is the truth: Marriage is a lifelong *commitment*. You don't quit whenever you feel like it.

3. Deciding whether to remain a virgin until marriage. The path you choose will have one of two side effects: pain or joy.

Once you give up your virginity, you can never get it back. Yes, you can totally recommit to God, but it won't be the same as waiting. If your friends pressure you into having sex before marriage, consider one girl's answer: "In five minutes, I can become like you. But try as hard as you can, you can never again become like me."[4] Wait until you are married. It is *not* tacky or outdated. You are not a dork or stupid if you are a virgin! These days if you are a virgin, it feels like you are a rare gem, like you are the only one out there. More and more teenagers are having sex before marriage, and even younger kids are starting at the age of eleven and twelve. It is not easy to stay committed when you are surrounded by the world's pressures and enticements, but you are not alone. I can name hundreds of people who are virgins or who waited until marriage. Sin's message deceives women worldwide. It says, "It is so worth it so don't wait any longer." The media has distorted the truth about sex. It is on television, in movies, in songs, and even in the clothing stores. However, just because wrong messages about sex are nearly drowning our society, you don't have to give in. Stand strong and choose to wait until marriage.

Sex Is Not Love

If you think that you will find love through sex, you won't. Sex is not the same as love nor does sex produce love. True love is:

Patient and kind. Love is not jealous or boastful or proud or rude. It does not demand its own way. It is not irritable, and it keeps no record of being wronged. It does not rejoice about injustice but rejoices whenever the truth wins out. Love never gives up, never loses faith, is always hopeful, and endures through every circumstance ... Love will last forever!

—1 Corinthians 13:1, 4–7 NLT

Note the difference between love and lust:

Love is patient: it gives	Lust is greedy: it takes
Love does not demand	Lust wants right now
Love is kind	Lust brings sorrow
Love is unconditional	Lust is conditional
Love is faithful	Lust waivers
Love never gives up	Lust quits when fulfilled
Love endures trials	Lust avoids trials
Love is selfless	Lust is self-centered

When a boy says, "If you love me then you will have sex with me," or persuades, "I love you so much, so will you have sex with me?" That is not love; it is lust! If he really loved you, then he would wait. Love is so much more than physical—it is a commitment and an action word. If I tell my husband I love him and then do not talk to him, he won't believe me. He shouldn't believe me if I treat him like that. Fortunately, we both have wedding bands symbolizing our love. When I look at my finger I can remember, "He does love me; he showed up that day, took vows, and committed his life to me." We proved our love to each other through marriage, not through pre-marital sex.

Guys may think having sex is the way to prove love, but that is a lie straight from the pit. You want a guy who will respect you, one who shares the same beliefs. A man who loves the Lord will look at you through Jesus' eyes. He will see you as a delicate and rare flower, not as a piece of meat. If you are in a relationship where you are yelled at, pressured to do things you don't want to, or disrespected in any way, get out of that relationship! Do not for one second think that you are unable to do anything about it. Look at him and just say, "It is over!" You are worth so much. Do not allow yourself to be treated like a piece of garbage.

We proved our love to each other through marriage, not through pre-marital sex. Guys may think having sex is the way to prove love, but that is a lie straigtht from the pit.

Consequences

The Bible commands us not to have sex outside of marriage. If you choose to anyway, you are in sin, and there are consequences for your actions. Here are five of many consequences:

1. *Guilt, shame, and regret.* Long-term consequences mostly occur in the woman. I know from experience that women are very emotional, and sex is a very emotional act. The emotional side effects of sex outside of marriage are horrendous. Problem areas include trust issues, fear of intimacy, rage, and feelings of worthlessness. All these will affect your future marriage.

2. *You can contract a* sexually transmitted disease (STD). According to several reports, half of all young Americans will contract an STD by the age of twenty-five. So many people, especially teenagers, are dying from STDs every year. Sadly, 60-80 percent of guys lie to girls about diseases just to get them in bed.[5] This is reality!

3. *You can become pregnant*. Approximately 40 percent of young women become pregnant before they reach twenty years of age. Every year, almost 1 million girls become pregnant.[6] You can use contraceptives, but none are 100 percent effective. I know girls who became pregnant while taking birth control pills. I know girls who became pregnant while using condoms. The only thing that will keep you from getting pregnant is abstinence. If you become pregnant, then you will be faced with many more difficult decisions. What will you do with your baby? What about the father? Will he be there to support you? There are so many questions and decisions. Are you ready to have a baby?

4. *Your relationship with the Lord will be hindered.* *"This is the message which we have heard from Him and declared to you, that God is light and in Him is no darkness at all. If we say that we have fellowship with Him, and walk in darkness, we lie and do not practice the truth. But if we walk in the light as He is in the light, we have fellowship with one another, and the blood of Jesus Christ His Son cleanses us from sin"* (1 John 1:5–7). You cannot practice sex outside of marriage and also follow the Lord. It doesn't work like that. You are either for Him or against Him. When Joseph was tempted to sleep with his master's

wife, he refused her and said, *"How then can I do this great wickedness, and sin against God?"* (Genesis 39:9). A hindered relationship with God should truly be the first and most important reason not to have sex outside of marriage. It breaks His heart.

5. *It will lead to death. "But each one is tempted when he is drawn away by his own desires and enticed. Then when desire has conceived, it gives birth to sin; and sin, when it is full grown, brings forth death"* (James 1:14–15). Jon Courson puts it best when he says, "Sin always brings forth death. Every time. Sin will kill relationships. It will destroy happiness. It will ruin health. When you want to show others how serious sin is and what sin does, the best thing you can do is take them to the Cross of Calvary and say, 'Look at this wonderful, perfect, loving Person and see Him on the Cross in agony and pain and blood. It was when Jesus became sin for us that He died, for sin *always* brings death.'"[7]

After recognizing some of the consequences that sex outside of marriage can bring, is it still worth it? Is all the pain and suffering worth it? Once you determine that it is not, I really want to encourage you to always be in the Word of God because Satan will try everything to make you fall. Make sure to set boundaries when you are dating or are engaged. Set the standard and really stick to it. Do not watch movies by yourselves in your boyfriend's room with the door closed and the lights off. It is so easy to give in to temptation if you make it easy. Don't even open the door to temptation. Don't play with fire if you don't want to get burned. In a later chapter, I will talk more about resisting temptation. So I pray that you will be prepared, that you will run from temptation, and that you will choose to wait to have sex until marriage.

chapter six

He's Worth Waiting For

Be anxious for nothing, but in everything by prayer and supplication, with thanksgiving, let your requests be made known to God.

—Philippians 4:6

We live in an instant age: fast food, text messages, online shopping, overnight shipping, and much more. Though we do at times experience waiting, life for Americans has become convenient and quick. We are not a patient generation, and in a world consumed with being instantly gratified, no areas are left untainted. The effects even reach our attitudes about sex. Society declares each of us should enjoy sex whenever we want and with whomever we want. And we wonder why it is so hard to wait. The world's counsel is, "Why enjoy sex later when you can have it right now? Why get married, when you can try it out by living together? If it feels good, go for it. Why wait? Waiting is no fun." Waiting is not fun, but the reward of waiting is so very worth it. God has so many blessings ready to pour into your precious life. He created sex and He created your perfect match, but are you willing to wait for the one God has for you? Yes!!!

When it comes to relationships, waiting is the last word we want to hear. We women want to have someone hold, love, and cherish us. The Lord offers what we desire, but it takes waiting for His timing. The psalmist writes, *"May He grant you according to your heart's desire, and fulfill all your purpose"* (Psalm 20:4). If you look to your flesh or to the world to fulfill your longings, you will only find corruption and destruction, but if you seek the Lord, you will find ultimate satisfaction and complete fulfillment.

A Perfect Match

> *And the* Lord *God said, "It is not good that man should be alone; I will make him a helper comparable to him." Out of the ground the* Lord *God formed every beast of the field and every bird of the air, and brought them to Adam to see*

what he would call them. And whatever Adam called each living creature that was its name. So Adam gave names to all cattle, to the birds of the air, and to every beast of the field. But for Adam there was not found a helper comparable to him. And the LORD God caused a deep sleep to fall on Adam, and he slept; and He took one of his ribs, and closed up the flesh in its place. Then the rib which the LORD God had taken from man He made into a woman, and He brought her to the man. And Adam said: "This is now bone of my bones and flesh of my flesh; she shall be called Woman, because she was taken out of Man."

—Genesis 2:18–23

*God looked at what had He created and saw that everything was good. ... But when God saw Adam all alone, He said that was **not** good.*

We read in the first chapter of Genesis that God spent six days creating the heavens, the earth, and everything in them. He created the stars, the sun, the moon, and all the creatures roaming the earth and filling the waters. Then God created man. God looked at what He had created and saw that everything was good. The morning and the evening were good; the seas and the earth were good; the grass and the trees were good; the seasons, the days, and the years were good; the lions roaming the earth, the birds soaring through the blue sky, and the whales swimming through the deep ocean were good. But when God saw Adam all alone, He said that was *not* good. Adam was alone; he needed a helpmate.

Adam had God to walk with, a garden to tend, and animals

to play with, but God saw that none were comparable to him. *Comparable* here means a counterpart, one formed from Adam who would be a perfect resemblance of his person. Adam did not have someone comparable to him and God knew that. In fact, God knew Adam's need even before Adam did. God also knows every single one of your needs. He knows how much sunsets make you want to sing, how a warm fire makes you want to curl up in a snug blanket, and how rain outsides makes you want to splash in the puddles. He knows how much you love singing into a hairbrush in front of the mirror and pretending to be a famous singer. He knows how much you love watching cute fairy-tale movies, hoping a prince will sweep you off your feet. He knows how much you like to dance in your car while driving down the highway. He knows what makes you joyful, sad, or angry. He knows your heart's deepest longings. He knew that Adam was alone and needed someone comparable to him. God desired to fulfill Adam's need, and He did. God knows that you desire to be married. He knew what feelings you would have this very second, even before you were created; and He desires to fulfill your needs.

We read in Genesis 2:19–20 that God gave Adam a job. He brought every created animal to Adam for him to name. Perhaps Adam began, "Okay, Mr. and Mrs. Hippo. And here we have Mr. and Mrs. Goat. Oh, and there is Mr. and Mrs. Pig, Mr. and Mrs. Rhino, and Mr. and Mrs. Gorilla." When do you think Adam finally realized he was a *Mr.* without a *Mrs.*? God did not give Adam this job because He was bored or because He needed to keep Adam preoccupied. God gave Adam this task with a purpose! He was making Adam aware of his need. Adam was in the garden having a great time. He got to walk with God every day and hang out with all those amazing creatures, but there was something missing. Adam could not really talk to the animals.

He had no companion, no one like him. When he began to name the animals and saw that there was a female and a male of each, he must have realized he did not have a female to go along with him. God made Adam aware of his need, and He makes us aware of ours too.

I probably first thought about my need in kindergarten. Because my parents happened to go to the same kindergarten, I thought I would meet my husband there too. But at that age boys do not care about finding a spouse. They are more excited about mud, getting dirty, and playing with trucks. In kindergarten, girls have cooties and boys have cooties; no one is thinking about marriage. That all changes in junior high. Kids experience new feelings as they notice people holding hands while walking together. They too may begin to long for that kind of attention and affection. In junior high every time I went anywhere, I would see a guy put his arm around his girlfriend or wife. For me, every couple stood out like a neon billboard sign. It started to drive me crazy because I did not have a significant other. I did not know what it was like to be a couple. God made me aware of my need to have someone like that. I'm sure if you are reading this book, then you are probably aware of your need. Perhaps you desire to develop a relationship with the opposite sex. Well, hold on and let's look at what happens next; it is monumental.

"But for Adam there was not found a helper comparable to him. And the LORD God caused a deep sleep to fall on Adam, and he slept" (Genesis 2:20–21). In naming the animals, Adam realized that there was none comparable to him, so what did he do? He went to sleep. Adam did not go out searching for his match. He did not join a dating service, he did not go to the mall, and he did not go to a club. He did not say, "Thanks God for making me aware of my need; now I am going to find my helper. I am going

to search for her myself." Could you imagine the result if Adam had tried to find a wife on his own? Adam was the only human being on the face of the earth. He could have looked at his possible prospects and found a gorilla to be the closest match. Adam could have looked at the animals and tried to make a relationship work with one of them, but that would have been ridiculous. Listen, if you try to find your own match and are willing to go to any length to get him, the results could be as outlandish as our example of Adam. If you determine "I don't care, I am going to make this work," you will be looking for your counterpart among quite a variety of animals. Most likely, you will find yourself with a beast, not the best.

Before I was married, I questioned whether every guy was "the one." I desperately wanted to know who I was going to marry. I would wonder, "Is it him? What about him? This guy? No, that one has to be it. What about …?" If you are like me, then you know what I am talking about. For those who are searching, there are varieties of dating services promising to help you meet "the one." If fact, there are many ways to try to find the man of your dreams, but nothing of your own doing will help, only God's plan will. So instead of searching, go to sleep!

You don't have to strive to find a husband. Striving and taking over for God will only make situations worse. God knows your need and He will meet it. Don't be looking for the man of your dreams because you might look right past him. Look to God; He will bring you to your perfect match. Close your eyes and pray, "Okay God, my emotions are out of control. I desire so badly to get married, but I don't want to force things. I want You to make it happen. So I give my desires to You, and no matter what, I am going to wait for Your timing. Equip me with the strength to wait and endure."

One day, out of desperation, I wrote a letter to God. My emotions had finally peaked and I could hardly go on. I desired to get married more than I ever had and I could hardly focus. I prayed that God would take over my life and give me strength to wait for the man He had for me. He equipped me with that strength and He immediately became the center of my attention. Then I became more concerned with how to imitate God than with whom to marry. Look to God, and let Him be the center of your attention.

Why Is Nothing Happening?

> *And He took one of his ribs, and closed up the flesh in its place. Then the rib which the* Lord *God had taken from man He made into a woman, and He brought her to the man. And Adam said: "This is now bone of my bones and flesh of my flesh; she shall be called Woman, because she was taken out of Man."*
>
> —Genesis 2:21–23

When Adam went to sleep, God did not. God did not yawn and say, "Okay, now that Adam is sleeping, I am going to rest too." No, He continued working in Adam's life.

After you give God your desires and ask Him to work, sometimes it can feel like nothing is happening. You may surrender your desires to Him, but find that no one is interested in you even though you may have thought that God would provide a match soon after. It is easy to feel like God is sleeping, but those feelings are incorrect. All through high school, I was faced with that very situation. I never had a serious boyfriend. It seemed the guy I liked never liked me back, and then the guys that liked me I wasn't interested in. I had a limited view of how God was working. Have you ever felt like that? Like nothing is happening in your life? Maybe you have never had a close relationship with a guy. The times when I did not, I convinced myself I was undesirable. I practically pulled out my hair wondering why no one liked me. And then one day I was sure I had met "the one." Boy, was I wrong.

On the first day of summer camp, my friend Jenn and I sat outside contemplating what we should do for the afternoon. We were tired, hot, and hungry, so we sat on the curb in front of the recreation room to wait for lunch. Using the water from her water bottle, Jenn began drawing a flower on the asphalt in front us. She was intent upon her artwork when four boys came running up. The leader jumped on Jenn's water flower, kicked his leg as high as he could, and shouted, "Does that impress you ladies?" Then, as quickly as they had come, the group ran away chuckling. I nervously laughed, but Jenn was in shock at how rudely they had ruined her artwork.

"Who were those boys?" I asked.

"They came with our church," Jenn answered.

I had never seen them before. When lunch began, Jenn and I got up and made our way to the dining hall for some gourmet camp food. We entered the cafeteria, and were met by a burst of loud chatter and clanging dishes ringing throughout the large room. By the time we arrived, seats at all the tables were filled. There was only one table in the whole room with two empty seats; it just happened to be the one where the artwork-destroying boys sat. We were forced to sit and eat with them. I thought it was a huge mistake because all they talked about were girls who had crushes on them, and girls who had cooties. I would have rather sat outside, but we were stuck. Jenn and I ate quietly while the boys continued their loud, obnoxious conversation. Before we knew it, lunch was over and the boys left.

The next morning devotions were scheduled to be in the sanctuary. I went early by myself, having no idea what I would find. The boy who had asked if we were impressed with his high kick was leading worship. I was taken aback. Here I had thought this obnoxious guy probably never went to church, but he was leading other high school students into the Lord's throne room. I talked to him after the service, and we became friends. I still thought he was obnoxious and loud, but he was different from my first impression of him.

I have always loved romantic stories. I love hearing about how my parents or other couples met. I love watching fairy-tale movies where the prince comes and sweeps his princess off her feet. I had always wanted a long romantic story of how my future husband and I would meet. I also desired specific traits for the kind of guy I planned to marry some day. Actually, someone had advised me to write those traits down and then never settle for anything less. When I met that guy at camp, I was convinced I would never see him again, but I saw him every week at church. We found ourselves meeting in unexpected places. I actually began to like him because I realized he fit every single quality on my list. He seemed perfect. I never planned our wedding or anything, but I really thought that he was whom God had for me. To this day, I don't know if he ever liked me. I prayed constantly that God would work it out. More than anything, I wanted him to be "the one." We could have had a romantic story of how we had met and kept running into each other in the most unusual places. It made me believe it was a work of God. He had every quality I was looking for, every quality I needed, or so I thought. But nothing happened. He wasn't pursuing me and never expressed any romantic feelings. We were nothing more than friends. I tried everything to get over it. I would tell my close friends that I was over him, but I wasn't. I thought saying it aloud would help, but it did not. I tried so hard to get him out of my head, but I could not stop thinking about him. I even tried to like other guys, but none were as amazing as he was.

A few years later, he ended up meeting the woman that the Lord had created for him. I ran into him once at a friend's wedding and he told me how he was going to propose to her. About six months later, they were married. I could see how God had specifically designed them for each other and how I wasn't designed for him and he wasn't designed for me. It took almost five years for me to finally realize he wasn't the guy God had for me. However, it wasn't anything I did that allowed me to move on. It was God's promise of someone better. In His perfect timing, He would bring me to His best.

I know so many girls who have felt the same way. These are girls who like a guy seemingly forever, but the guy never returns the same feelings. What about you, can you relate to this story? Are you head over heels for an amazing guy, one who has all the perfect qualities, but one with whom nothing is happening? Do you feel like God isn't working? I wonder if Adam ever questioned the way God was working. We don't know what Adam was thinking, but we know God was working in Adam's life, and He is working every moment of every day in your life.

Maybe you feel desperate because nothing is happening right now. Maybe you have gone through relationship after relationship and none are working out. Whether you see God in your situation or not, He is still on the throne and He has your best interest in mind. While you are waiting, God is working. During those long years of agonizing over one guy, I did not realize that God was actually doing something else altogether. When we feel like God is not working in our lives, that may be when He is working most.

Instead of spending time wondering why nothing is happening, ask God, "How can I be more like You?" When your focus on the present situation is so intense, there isn't room for God. I agonized over why nothing was happening, when instead my focus should have been on God. It is so easy to get caught up in our own present situation, to think God is not working in our lives. When we girls don't have a boyfriend it is all too easy to throw a pity party. That is what happens when we focus on ourselves. This tendency, however, is not only found in girls.

When we place our focus on God, we become less worried about the work it feels like He isn't doing. God is working and He is going to amaze with the work that He does.

A man once shared with me he wasn't fully convinced God had only created one woman for him. Nevertheless, he was still worried he had already blown his opportunity somewhere. He was probably in his late thirties and had never been married. Unfortunately, he was more concerned with figuring out whether or not God creates only one right person for each of us than he was about living his life to please God. He was so focused on his worry that love would pass him by, that he was missing the peace we find in trusting God's perfect timing. When we place our focus on God, we become less worried about the work it feels like He isn't doing. God is working and He is going to amaze you with the work He does.

I just want to encourage you to focus on the Lord and ask Him, "What do You desire to do with me right now?" and "How can I be more like You?" Focus on spending time in His Word and deepening your relationship with Him. Quit looking at your present situation. God has the perfect man for you, but you need to surrender this season to God and simply sit at His feet. Enjoy the journey and remember it was when Adam fell asleep that God began to work.

Perfectly Fit

Adam awoke to the most beautiful creature he had ever seen. I wish I could have watched his face light up when his gaze locked on her. His countenance must have glowed like a groom catching the first glance of his beautiful bride. I love seeing that look! He was so amazed at what God had done, he could hardly contain himself. Adam had *waited* while God was working, and now he was ready to enjoy his bride that God had *brought* to him.

This part of the story is so intriguing to me because God brought Eve to Adam. Adam wasn't running around looking for her. While he waited, God was shaping, forming, and creating Eve into a beautiful, flawless, amazing woman. God handcrafted her character brighter than gold. Sin had not entered the world yet, and Eve was perfect. She had no complaints about her appearance. She did not think she was too fat or fuss that her hair wasn't just right. She was a perfectly designed creature in a perfect world.

When Adam laid eyes on Eve he declared, *"This is now bone of my bones and flesh of my flesh; she shall be called Woman, because she was taken out of Man"* (Genesis 2:23). Eve was Adam's perfect match. In 2 Corinthians 8:14, Paul writes about the body of Christ filling each other's needs, saying, *"at this time your abundance may supply their lack, that their abundance also may supply your lack—that there may be equality."* This relationship works with a man and a woman too. Where Adam was weak Eve was strong, and where Eve was weak Adam was strong. There was equality.

I will never forget the first day that I met Dan Leitz, my precious husband. For the first time I did not ask, "Is it him?" Sparks did not fly and it wasn't love at first sight. We don't have a fairy-tale story. It was just like any other day and he was just another friend. Surprisingly, he thought the same of me. I didn't walk in the room with a glow of light surrounding me. In fact, we weren't even searching for the person God had for us because we were still sleeping. God wasn't finished with us, so we weren't ready to know we had been made for each other. I actually went on a mission's trip to Russia two days after first meeting Dan, and then did not see him for a month. During that time I never thought about him or worried if he liked me. I was sleeping. But God awoke me and brought me to him just a month later. I finally was at that point where I wasn't looking for my future husband and I did not have a list of qualities that had to be met. I was satisfied with the season I was in. So God said, "Perfect, just where I have wanted you." I believe with my whole heart that Dan and I were specifically created for each other. He is my other half. He fills in where I leave off. His strengths are my weaknesses and my strengths are his weaknesses. There is equality. God designed me for him and him for me, and we both realized this the second time we hung out.

Our relationship is a miraculous work of God. We began dating within a few weeks of knowing each other, and we were engaged about a month and a half later. Here is the amazing part of our story: We never rushed ahead of God. It was all in His perfect timing. When Adam first saw Eve, he did not say, "Are you sure God? Is this really Your will? Give me a sign to show me this is really who You have for me." No, Adam said, "Whoa, bone of my bones and flesh of my flesh!" Adam knew! He just simply knew and he went for it. She became his wife that instant. God did a miraculous work in Adam and Eve's lives, and He did the same with Dan and me. I never had to strive after Dan or try to make it work. It just happened. God brought me to Dan and said, "This is good. This is My best for you!" Your story may unfold differently than ours. It may take you a lot longer to wake up; you may date for a long time before you get engaged. I don't know, but I know God's timing is perfect and I know that God works differently in every person's life. So don't think that because God worked this way in my life that He is going to do the exact same with you. There is no example couple for everyone else to follow. God doesn't belong in a box. Surrender to Him, and allow Him to work His best in His way!

Giving Up for His Best

God has amazing plans for your life (I can never say that enough). He is working in you and in your future husband. He is molding and shaping you into a beautiful woman after His heart. Listen, if you desire to be married, give that desire to God. You are aware of your need and God wants to give you all your desires. *"No good thing will He withhold from those who walk uprightly"* (Psalm 84:11). He has created the perfect man for you. If you desire to marry God's best for you, it will take a season of waiting. So if you hear our world declare, "If it feels good then do it," remember that God has a greater plan than something that just feels good. A marriage that God has ordained is worth waiting for. You will be blessed beyond your wildest dreams. Each of those other guys who I thought was the one would have never been able to treat me and look at me the way my husband does. They weren't created for me. God withheld those guys because they were not His best for me. I know that God does not withhold anything good from us. However, He does withhold things that are not good. Praise Him for that! Maybe if nothing is happening in your life right now, it is because God is withholding something that would not be good. You don't want a relationship, especially a marriage, that is not good.

I know that God does not withhold anything good from us. However, He does withhold things that are not good.

"But seek first the kingdom of God and His righteousness, and all these things shall be added to you" (Matthew 6:33). Keep God the center of your focus. The one He has for you is definitely worth waiting for.

chapter seven

Resisting Temptation

Be sober, be vigilant; because your adversary the devil walks about like a roaring lion seeking whom he may devour. Resist him, steadfast in the faith.

—1 Peter 5:8–9

As you can see in the verse on the previous page, Satan's ultimate goal is to destroy your life and take you with him to hell. His future is hell, he knows it, and he will do everything in his power to try to get as many people as he can to go there with him. *Vigilant* means to be watchful. "Watchful of what?" you might ask. Well, watchful of what the devil wants to do with your life. Look at what the Bible says to be watchful for:

> *... sexual immorality, impure thoughts, eagerness for lustful pleasure, idolatry, participation in demonic activities, hostility, quarreling, jealousy, outbursts of anger, selfish ambition, divisions, the feeling that everyone is wrong except those in your own little group, envy, drunkenness, wild parties, and other kinds of sin.*
>
> —Galatians 5:19–21 NLT

The Bible also says: *"Let me tell you again, as I have before, that anyone living that sort of life will not inherit the kingdom of God"* (Galatians 5:21 NLT).

If you are not on guard, it will be easy to fall into temptation. However, temptation can be resisted, and you are completely capable through Christ not to give in. It has been said that Christians are a lot like tea bags—you don't know what they're made of until you put them in hot water. Will you give in to the temptation or will you take a stand against it?

Long before I was married, an extremely tempting situation arose. I was working at a Starbucks Coffee shop where a handsome young man would frequently visit. Since I had only been working there a short time, I became really flustered each time he came in. It suddenly seemed I couldn't do anything correctly. It was embarrassing to stumble over my words and mess up his order.

Mr. Handsome was about 5' 8". He had dark eyes, dark wavy hair, dark skin, and was Australian. His accent was breathtaking. He was extremely captivating, so when I overheard that he was employed at another Starbucks but was transferring to the store where I worked, my heart leapt at the opportunity to get to know him better. Much to my disappointment, our shifts were scheduled at opposite times for the first four weeks, so I hardly saw him. Finally, my chance came—our first shift together. I was so nervous! My heart beat wildly every time he smiled at me. I could hardly concentrate because I was so distracted by him. Eventually, we started working together more often and learned to love talking about everything—from surfing to newly released movies. Soon I found out he was not a Christian; we had completely different beliefs. So I began to witness.

Since he lived right down the street from our work, there were a few times I gave him a ride home. I made sure that our conversations were only about the Lord. He was so interested and seemed so close to accepting Christ as his personal Savior. I gave him a Bible, took him to a Christian concert, and even persuaded him to come to church one time. I was so excited that this amazingly handsome guy was about to come to know Christ, mostly because I started to fall hard for him. I couldn't help it. He was such a gentleman, not to mention charming and handsome.

Up to then, I had never seriously dated, and I had always wanted my first serious relationship to be with the man I would marry. I hoped so badly that this guy would become a Christian. I knew I couldn't date someone who had different beliefs. The Lord was, and is, the love of my life; and He was, and is, my everything. How was I supposed to share a life with someone who didn't share my love for the Lord? I would be trying to live in the light with someone who could only live in the dark. Bright light and complete darkness cannot share the same space. I had been praying for a man after God's heart and I knew that if I waited, the Lord would bring me to him, *not* to a non-Christian. However, I really struggled with this temptation because my desire to have a boyfriend was greatly increasing. He eventually told me he was interested in me, and confessed to checking first thing each day to see if I was working the same shift. He said he always wanted to see me. My heart leapt at those words. I couldn't believe that this boy would even be interested in me. So you can imagine how this potential temptation became actual.

My co-workers weren't Christians, but they knew my standards. They were watching to see if I would settle for a non-Christian guy. My flesh wanted to experience a relationship, to hold his hand, and to be in love; but my spirit knew it would destroy me. I was in a battle. My feelings were out of control and I could hardly think straight. I would practically beat myself over the head wondering why I was falling for a non-Christian. My friends tried to talk me out of it, but nothing was working. I even tried to talk myself out of it, but that did not work either. Then the Lord spoke. During a church service, our pastor taught on these verses: *"Therefore we also, since we are surrounded by so great a cloud of witnesses, let us lay aside every weight and the sin which so easily ensnares us, and let us run with endurance the race that is set before us, looking unto Jesus, the author and finisher of our faith"* (Hebrews 12:1–2). My flesh wanted a relationship with this guy, but the Lord was asking me to lay aside every weight and the sin that so easily ensnares. So, right then, on October 1, 2003, I committed to stand for Christ, to proclaim Him as my King, and to follow His plan, knowing that it would be much greater than my own fleshly desires.

I recorded this commitment in my Bible and called my friend to share what the Lord had spoken—a relationship between us would never work out. Fortunately, nothing happened; we just remained friends. That phone call was a battle and a half for me. I wanted our relationship to work out so badly, but knew it could never last. He wasn't someone I wanted to marry, so what was the point of dating him? The relationship would have drawn me away from the Lord. A right relationship will draw us closer to the Lord, not farther away. We never hung out again and hardly ever worked together. I deleted his number from my phone so I wouldn't be tempted to call. I had to slam the door on this desire in order to keep Satan from getting a foothold. Resisting temptation and knowing you did not compromise by falling prey to the devil and his plans gives you a wonderful confidence. A great feeling of victory came from choosing God's plan for my life. Little did I know how great His plan would be. He blessed me with the most amazing man after His heart. If I had not been faithful (by the power of the Holy Spirit) to the Lord, I might have missed out on His best. I praise the Lord that I followed His way instead of my own!

I deleted his number from my phone so I wouldn't be tempted to call. I had to slam the door on this desire in order to keep Satan from getting a foothold.

Just like I did, through the power of the Lord, you have the capability and strength to resist temptation; you don't have to face them alone. Jesus also had to resist the flesh. He understands the battle and is with you to help, *"for in that He Himself has suffered, being tempted, He is able to aid those who are tempted"* (Hebrews

2:18). Resisting in our own strength can be ridiculously difficult. Trust me, I know. God is more than ready and willing to help us resist the temptation to date a non-Christian or to do anything else out of His will. Temptations will come; it is not a matter of if, but a matter of when. In his book, *I'm Going on a Diet Tomorrow (and other lies we tell ourselves)*, Greg Laurie writes, "The devil knows that one of the most effective ways to pull someone down is through the deadly and very effective ploy of compromise."[8] Since the beginning of time, the devil has twisted the truth, working to plant doubt in our minds. "Did God *really* say that?" he questions. Compromising by dating a non-Christian could end in destruction. Paul, inspired by the Holy Spirit, writes, *"Do not be unequally yoked together with unbelievers. For what fellowship has righteousness with lawlessness? And what communion has light with darkness?"* (2 Corinthians 6:14). When Satan tries to talk you into being unequally yoked, he is leading you into compromise; and, as in many other temptations, it begins in the mind. Be aware of thoughts like, "He is so cute," or "He is really nice. I could bring him to church and maybe he will get saved," or "I really like him and I can't help it." These thoughts begin the very slippery slope of compromise. If you feel conviction, it is the Holy Spirit warning you to run from the situation. Don't give in; you will be much better off. Pray, ask the Lord for strength, and He will give it to you. Here are six reasons why you should *not* give in to the temptations that *will* come your way.

1) It Will Break the Lord's Heart

"Then the Lord saw that the wickedness of man was great in the earth, and that every intent of the thoughts of his heart was only evil continually ... and He was grieved in His heart"

(Genesis 6:5–6). It hurts when a close friend stands you up or talks about you behind your back. It hurts when your friends ditch you to hang out with someone else. It hurts the Lord so much more when you turn your back on Him and walk away from His promises.

2) It Will Hinder Your Relationship with the Lord

When Samson decided to give in to temptation, the presence of the Lord left him (Judges 16:20). The Spirit of the Lord also departed from Saul when he gave in to his flesh (1 Samuel 16:14). The Lord, who is light, cannot dwell with darkness. When you decide to give in to temptation, God's blessing will not be upon you, and your relationship with Him will suffer. He tells us, *"each one is tempted when he is drawn away by his own desires and enticed. Then, when desire has conceived, it gives birth to sin; and sin, when it is full-grown, brings forth death"* (James 1:14–15). Giving in to temptation is just the beginning of the path to destruction.

3) It Can Ruin the Greater the Plan of God's Best for You

In the book of Numbers, we read that God instructed Moses to send one man from every Israelite tribe to spy out the land of Canaan. The men returned after forty days with a great report, carrying back amazing fruit and sharing how the land prospered, flowing with milk and honey. Moses decided Israel would go in and take over the territory, but the men who were sent to spy out the land feared the giants they saw there. They warned the Israelite warriors they would all be killed. Finally the Israelites determined not to take over the land of Canaan. The Bible records:

> *All the children of Israel complained against Moses and Aaron, and the whole congregation said to them, "If only we had died in the land of Egypt! Or if only we had died in this wilderness! Why has the LORD brought us to this land to fall by the sword, that our wives and children should become victims? Would it not be better for us to return to Egypt?"*
>
> —Numbers 14:2–3

God had delivered His people from the Egyptians, provided food and water for them in the desert, performed miracles and signs to preserve them, and finally promised them an amazing land; but they refused it. They didn't believe that God would give them Canaan, so they suffered the consequences—they did not enter in to enjoy the amazing blessings. Instead, they ended up wandering in the desert for forty years. The next generation, the Israelites' children, were able to enter the Promised Land; but if the Israelites had believed and trusted God, they could have enjoyed His blessings forty years earlier. Similarly, if you decide to give in to the temptations that look good now, you may not be able to receive His best. Wait and believe His promise.

4) It Will Destroy Your Witness

We are examples of Christ. We are His witnesses. Paul tells us that we *"shall receive power when the Holy Spirit has come upon you; and you shall be witnesses to Me in Jerusalem, and in all Judea and Samaria, and to the end of the earth"* (Acts 1:8).

When I was working for Starbucks, every employee there knew I was a Christian. If I had given in to the temptation of dating an unbeliever, I would have been a poor witness. They would have been quick to say, "Oh, she is like everyone else. What a hypocrite." Would you want to tell people about the promises of God and not believe them for yourself? People are watching, waiting to see how long it is before you give in to sin and compromise. If you resist temptation, people will see the Lord in you. Be a true witness for Christ.

5) It Is Sin

It is not a sin when you are faced with temptation. It is only a sin if you choose to give in to the temptation. Matthew records that even Jesus was tempted, *"Then Jesus was led up by the Spirit into the wilderness to be tempted by the devil"* (Matthew 4:1), but Jesus didn't give in. That may not seem a fair comparison because Jesus was perfect. Remember, though, Jesus became a man and He didn't eat for forty days. He was starving. When Satan suggested He turn rocks into bread, of course Jesus was tempted to eat, but He chose not to sin.

David, Israel's king and a man after God's own heart, also dealt with temptation. He was lingering at home when he should have been out in battle. He saw beautiful Bathsheba, sent for her, and got what he wanted. Bathsheba was already married and to make matters worse she became pregnant by David. Trying to cover up his lustful act, David ended up adding sin to sin. Continuing to give in to temptation leads us to become slaves to sin. That is what happened to David. Though deceit may only begin with a white lie, it is hard to stop once the cycle has begun. Another lie must be told to cover the first one. If you read the rest of David's story (2 Samuel 11–12), he truly repented and God still used him in great ways, but David still had to suffer the consequences of his sin.

6) *It Will Rob You of Joy*

There is no joy in sin. You *will* be miserable. *"He who sows iniquity will reap sorrow"* (Proverbs 22:8). When David sinned, he lost his joy. Guilt plagued his conscience and he worried about trying to cover his mistakes. David shares his feelings in Psalm 51:

> *Have mercy upon me, O God, according to Your lovingkindness; according to the multitude of Your tender mercies, blot out my transgressions. Wash me thoroughly from my iniquity, and cleanse me from my sin. For I acknowledge my transgressions, and my sin is always before me. Against You, You only, have I sinned, and done this evil in Your sight. ... Create in me a clean heart, O God, and renew a steadfast spirit within me. Do not cast me away from Your presence, and do not take Your Holy Spirit from me. Restore to me the joy of Your salvation, and uphold me by Your generous Spirit. Then I will teach transgressors Your ways, and sinners shall be converted to You. Deliver me from the guilt of bloodshed, O God, the God of my salvation, and my tongue shall sing aloud of Your righteousness.*
>
> —Psalm 51:1–4,10–14

I pray you would choose not to give in when temptation comes your way. Be a woman after God's own heart and follow Him, not your fleshly desires. Choose what is right, not what is easy. It is never worth giving in to temptation. James 1:12 says, *"Blessed is the man who endures temptation."* You will be blessed because the rest of the verse says, *"For when he has been approved, he will receive the crown of* life *which the Lord has promised to those who love Him."* Temptation can be endured and the reward is greater than you know! Alistair Begg, senior pastor of Parkside Church in Cleveland, says to Christian women struggling with dating a non-Christian, "You can cry now because you've lost him, or you can cry later because you've got him (after you have married)."[9]

Imprisoned

It is interesting to compare the stories of Joseph and Samson. Both men were faced with similar tempting situations. When Joseph was seventeen years old, his envious older brothers sold him as a slave to Midianite traders. They, in turn, sold him as a slave to Potiphar, a powerful Egyptian ruler (Genesis 39:1–13). Although Joseph had dedicated his life to the Lord, it probably seemed like everything was going wrong. He had dreamt that his brothers and family would bow down to him. Instead of honoring him, his brothers sold him as a slave. If I were in Joseph's position, I would be wondering what God's plan was. I'm sure it would not be fitting with my own idea of what should happen. I would ask, "Why do I have to go through this? I thought I would be in a place of power." But amazingly, it was through Joseph's captivity that God's glory was maximized. God was with Joseph's every step, and at just the right time He made him to prosper.

Interestingly, one of Joseph's most difficult temptations came when he was minding his own business. While he worked,

Potiphar's wife began to "cast longing eyes on him." Day after day, she threw herself upon Joseph and boldly demanded that he "lie" with her. Her advances probably seemed both flattering and shallow. It would require little effort for Joseph to satisfy his own flesh; all he had to do was agree. On the other hand, giving in to this temptation would be sinning against God.

Think about a time you were tempted. Was it easy to say no? Did you end up giving in? Can you remember the intense feelings and strong emotions? I do. When that amazingly good-looking young man found interest in me, my hormones raged out of control. My flesh was screaming at me because it desired to be with this guy and to be held by him. I believe it was difficult for Joseph to say no, but he knew what he had to do. He knew that the Lord was greater than his fleshly desires and would greatly exceed his own way. Joseph relied on the promises of God. When you are faced with difficult situations, always remember the promises of God, rely on them, and choose His way, not yours.

We are assured that *"the temptations in your life are no different from what others experience. ... God is faithful. He will not allow the temptation to be more than you can stand. When you are tempted, he will show you a way out so that you can endure"* (1 Corinthians 10:13 NLT). There will always be a way of escape, but you have to be willing to choose that way, and Joseph did just that. He refused his master's wife. His flesh was probably screaming as this woman threw herself at him. Acting wisely and quickly, Joseph fled. He ran as fast as he could from the situation. When faced with temptation, we cannot afford to linger, doubt, or even take time to think. We must run! Further from the temptation, Joseph probably felt relief. He had gained the victory and honored God.

Joseph faced temptation and chose to obey the Lord. Samson, also another Israelite, had also been called by God even before he was born (read Judges 13). Samson, however, pursued his fleshly desires, and ended up getting exactly what he wanted. Although the Lord strictly commanded that his people not intermarry with other races, Samson demanded a Philistine woman as his wife. As we will see, only problems came from that choice. Note Samson's fleshly reactions in each of the following situations.

When his wife was tormented by Philistine men because of a riddle, Samson went down in his strength and killed them. When Samson's father-in-law thought he hated his daughter (Samson's wife), he gave her to Samson's best man and would not permit Samson to see her. Drama. So Samson took foxes, lit their tails on fire, and sent them to the Philistine land where they set fire to all the corn, vineyards, and olive trees. The Philistines were so angered by this that they burned Samson's wife and her father. Samson then took revenge and killed these Philistines. Can you recognize a nonstop battle here? Samson was led by his desire. He wanted a wife, so that is what he got; he wanted revenge, so that is what he got. God had blessed Samson with great strength, and the Philistines knew that he could physically defeat any man. However, as we focus on the next chapter of his life, we see that despite all Samson's muscle, his weakness in another area would completely undo him (read Judges 16:4–21).

Samson loved a deceitful Philistine woman, and when his enemies offered Delilah money for the secret of his strength, she accepted. Samson's Nazarite vow restricted cutting hair (Judges 13:5). If he did, the vow would be broken and he would lose his strength. He knew that, but he still ended up revealing to a deceiving woman the secret of his strength. Three times, she manipulated Samson to compromise his secret, and three times he lied to her. You would think that Samson would have recognized her schemes by the third time. But he didn't. My mom says men are suckers for a pretty face. The Bible explains, *"She pestered him daily with her words and pressed him, so that his soul was vexed to death"* (Judges 16:16). Samson became wearied by her complaining, but instead of leaving her, he gave in to the temptation because he "loved" this woman. When Samson fully gave in, he lost his strength and was finally overcome by the Philistine men. They gouged out his eyes and threw him in prison. Both Joseph and Samson were tempted by beautiful women, but Joseph's story ended differently, as he was blessed for his obedience.

Joseph dealt with temptation by fleeing, but when Potiphar's wife turned against him, he still ended up being punished, remaining in prison for years. So we learn that if you make the wrong decision like Samson, you will be imprisoned, but if you make the right decision like Joseph, you will still be imprisoned. How confusing! I have found that after choosing the right way, the enemy comes to whisper lies to make me feel imprisoned anyway, and I begin to wonder if I have made the wrong choice. When I refused to give in to my Starbucks guy friend, he returned to his last girl. They came in almost every

We learn that if you make the wrong decision like Samson, you will be imprisoned, but if you make the right decision like Joseph, you will still be imprisoned. How confusing!

day, and I felt like he was trying to make me jealous. Sometimes it worked. Every once in a while I wondered if I had made the wrong choice or lost out on a great relationship. That was the enemy lying to me. I had made the right choice and God was going to reward me, but it was still tough.

When friends ask you to a party and you say no, or when that guy you like asks you to go to his house to spend time alone, you cannot listen to the devil's whispers. Don't listen to your friends when they try to make fun of you or call you names. Don't listen to the guy who tries to convince you that you made a wrong choice. You may feel like you are imprisoned, but resist and be encouraged because these two stories don't end with men in prison.

Joseph, after being in prison for years, still held to the Lord's promises. He knew that the Lord had great plans in store for him. Joseph became second in command in all Egypt. His dreams came true. Because of his position, Joseph's brothers ended up bowing down to him. Joseph made the right decision by not giving in to temptation, and even though he went to prison, his final reward was greater than he could imagine. When you choose to wait for the man whom God has for you, no matter what, you will be blown away by what the Lord will do.

For the most part, Samson's life dwindled away after prison. His hair grew back, along with his strength, and he ended up defeating the Philistines, but his life was taken along with theirs. If you feel imprisoned after making the right choice, know that it will only be for a short season. God's timing is perfect and the rewards are so worth it. Choose to run away from temptation and like Joseph be exalted; if you give in like Samson, you will be defeated. Resist temptation, choose God's plan, and wait.

Choosing the Right Path, Not the Easy Path

"My brethren, count it all joy when you fall into various trials, knowing that the testing of your faith produces patience. But let patience have its perfect work, that you may be perfect and complete, lacking nothing" (James 1:2–4). Choosing the right path is like swimming against the current or walking opposite in a huge crowd. It can seem impossible. Joey Buran, former Pipe Master's surfing champion and present pastor of Worship Generation, shared in one of his messages, "I would rather live having the worst day of my life as a Christian than live the best day of my life without Christ." He is a man who has walked the right path with God, not the easy path with Satan.

Remember Job? Let's take a look at his life. *"There was a man in the land of Uz, whose name was Job; and that man was blameless and upright, and one who feared God and shunned evil"* (Job 1:1). Satan took everything away from this God-fearing man, in hopes that Job would turn from God. Job had two choices: he could curse God and end all the pain and suffering or he could bless God and endure the pain and suffering. Job must have been very tempted to say those few words to curse God. Job had lost his seven sons, three daughters, all his livestock (oxen, donkeys, sheep), and all of his servants in the same day. But what did Job do? He said, *"'Naked I came from my mother's womb, and naked shall I return there. The Lord gave, and the Lord has taken away; blessed be the name of the Lord.' In all this Job did not sin nor charge God with wrong"* (Job 1:21–22). How amazing that Job did not curse God. Next, Satan *"struck Job with painful boils from the sole of his foot to the crown of his head"* (Job 2:7).

Satan really wanted Job to compromise and to give in. To top it off, Job's wife advised, *"Curse God and die"* (Job 2:9). Job lost his possessions, children, health, and now his wife had turned against him. She became a tool of Satan when she spoke those words. However, through all this, Job never chose the easy path. Instead, he blessed God and *endured* the pain and suffering. In the end, God blessed Job with twice as much as he had originally. If Job had cursed God, he might not have received anything back. He would have become Satan's tool.

What do you want to become—a tool of Satan or an instrument of God? *"Watch and pray, lest you enter into temptation. The spirit indeed is willing, but the flesh is weak"* (Matthew 26:41). Your spirit is willing to choose the right path, but your flesh is ready at all moments to choose the wrong path. Both roads lead to a different place: eternal life or eternal damnation. The apostle Paul says, *"And I know that nothing good lives in me, that is, in my sinful nature. I want to do what is right, but I can't. I want to do what is good, but I don't. I don't want to do what is wrong, but I do it anyway"* (Romans 7:18–19 NLT). It is sin in us creating a passion for worldly things. Satan made what the world offers fun and exciting, but it is also temporary; it only lasts a moment and then ends in destruction. So True!

So next time you face an extreme temptation, remember to pray for God's strength to make the right decision. Don't be discouraged. If you feel imprisoned or are worried that you might have made the wrong choice, remember how Joseph ran and was later exalted. Remember the anguish and regret that followed David's choice to give in. Remember how Samson's life ended when he gave in. Remember how Job endured and was later replenished with twice as much. There is one more thing to remember: God has an amazing plan for you. He wants to give you His best. *"Delight yourself also in the* L*ORD, and He shall give you the desires of your heart"* (Psalm 37:4). When you resist temptation, you will be blessed.

chapter eight

Incorruptible Beauty

Do not let your adornment be merely outward—arranging the hair, wearing gold, or putting on fine apparel—rather let it be the hidden person of the heart, with the incorruptible beauty of a gentle and quiet spirit, which is very precious in the sight of God.

—1 Peter 3:3–4

love this ♡

What gets a guy's attention? Is it how you act, what you say, or how much you flirt? What is it that attracts a guy to a girl? Is it the way she holds herself, her character, the way she looks, or sadly, how easy she is? The media declares that looks are most important, while modern magazines manage to talk about our bodies in a variety of articles. Teen magazines showcase titles like "Look pretty," "Make over your body," "405 ways to look hot," "Which beauty look was made for you?" The world declares that image matters more than character. Even more depressing is how often we women buy in to what they say. Young women quickly assume that their significance is directly related to their shape or size. Even worse, young women believe giving up their bodies and their hearts is the best way to become desirable to the opposite sex.

Why does the world teach these principles? It knows that guys are visual and sex sells. The world wants you to look hot, have the perfect skin, show as much of it as you can, and have the perfect body shape; otherwise, you may never get a guy's attention. Remind yourself over and over that this is a lie straight from hell. Models and movie stars are all unreasonable examples. If we strive to model ourselves after this ideal, we will only be disappointed that our features are less than perfect. Instead, let's talk about the different kinds of beauty that are flowing from all women's lives. Let's talk about beauty that will fade and beauty that will last.

Dressed to Impress

How do you dress? Do you believe what the world says—that looks are most important? What goes through your mind when you are trying on your new dress, skirt, or shirt? What is the motivation behind the way you dress? Do you want to look nice, do you want to get that guy's attention, or do you even care? How much time do you spend in front of the mirror? Would it devastate you more to forget your homework or to wake up late and not have enough time to spend on your appearance?

Today, fashion and trends are extremely important to young women, and many stores target teenage girls. I look around and see how mini skirts, halter tops, strapless shirts, low-cut jeans, and naked mid-drifts are the hottest fashions. Magazines say that you need to buy these types of clothes to look attractive. Girls long for the attention and attraction of a young man, and so the world offers ways to get that attention. How? By wearing revealing clothes and spending more time perfecting the way you look. But that will not attract the type of guy you desire.

Right before my freshman year of high school I started to blossom and many guys started to notice. I was so embarrassed by my body because I still wanted to be a tomboy. I wore sweatshirts, baggy pants, and skate shoes. I remember going to school one day, and to my surprise, two other guys in my class were wearing the same outfit as me. I couldn't believe how much I wanted to dress in boy clothes. But I was boy crazy, and dressing the way I did never got me the attention I desired. I was one of the "bros" to almost all of my guy friends. I loved surfing, skateboarding, and snowboarding, so I fit in with all these types of guys. But they all looked at me as only a friend, nothing more. I wanted to be more than just a friend, but in this, I was trying to feed both my flesh and my spirit.

You see, I wanted a boyfriend badly, but I was also passionate about only dating the guy I would marry. Desiring both made life really difficult. One had to go, so I tried to get a boyfriend.

I read girl magazines and listened to what my friends said about attracting the opposite sex. I took all the advice that I could and started wearing revealing clothes—short skirts, tight shirts, spaghetti-strap tops, and low-cut jeans.

My friends' advice worked amazingly well, and I was getting all the attention I longed for, immediately. I was so excited when guys started looking at me in a different way. They were talking about me and wanting to be around me. But these guys were not Christians and were not looking for any kind of commitment, only sex with no attachment. That was what my outward appearance was asking for. So while the guys at school were drooling, those at church were turning their heads the other direction. What I quickly realized is dressing provocatively only leads to disaster and a broken heart. Instead of being one of the "bros," I became a piece of meat, another girl guys would bet on to see how far they could get. Praise the Lord that I was protected by Him during that time and nothing happened. When you dress to reveal your body, you declare yourself easy bait. After a guy receives what he wants, he will be done with you and move on to the next challenge. Sadly, so many young girls are deceived.

I went to high school summer camp one year where one of the guy counselors shared that girls don't realize the effect their bodies have on guys' minds. As we sat at the pool, he explained that when guys see too much skin, they will picture that girl naked. I never knew that before and was amazed that guys really do struggle with girls' choices of seducing apparel. Really wrap your mind around that fact and grasp the reality of it. Like I said at the beginning of this chapter, guys are visual. Wearing revealing clothes will draw superficial attention.

The way a woman dresses will determine the kind of attention she will receive and the kind of relationship she will find. The kind of bait you throw out will determine what you will catch. *"Those who live only to satisfy their own sinful nature will harvest decay and death from that sinful nature"* (Galatians 6:8 NLT). What do you want: to attract a guy to your body or to your heart? Here is a story that will give you an idea of what I am talking about.

After grocery shopping in Costco, my husband and I sat down for lunch. Right next to our table was a man eating his meal and boldly staring at a young girl sitting opposite him one table over. He looked like he was over 30, while the young woman was probably in high school. The whole time we sat there, he was just staring at her and drooling. He wouldn't even look down at his food because he was so mesmerized by her appearance. This young woman's strapless shirt and short jean skirt were asking for that kind of attention. The whole time she was fiddling with her cell phone so I have no idea if she realized that this older man was checking her out. I mentioned this to my husband and he started watching too. This guy's friend called to him and he wouldn't move.

The way a woman dresses will determine the kind of attention she will receive and the kind of relationship she will find. The kind of bait you throw out will determine what you will catch.

This guy was most likely violating this young girl in his mind. He might have even gotten a glance at her underwear because of the way she was sitting. This is disgusting to me because I would never want a gross older man looking at me and violating me in his mind, and I know most of you probably wouldn't either. But I wonder how many times I could have received that same kind of attention, but like that girl, had no idea. If she were wearing a longer skirt or maybe pants and a less revealing shirt or a sweatshirt, would that same guy keep staring? My husband said he most definitely would not. There would be no room for the man's mind to wander; he would see a modest girl, not a bunch of skin. When you give a guy even a hint of seduction by what you wear, he will devour it up. Is that what you want? Do you want guys after you only for their pleasure? Do you want older men staring at you, undressing you with their eyes? I sure don't! When I realized the attention I was bringing in, I quickly changed my ways. Not one guy wanted anything past my body. What I wore on the outside was so much different than my heart. I only attracted guys who could care less about my heart. This is what you will attract too if you choose to dress in revealing clothes.

As you pick out your wardrobe, I pray that you will fully understand how visual guys are and how easily they are stumbled. It only takes a look and then a thought and a guy can lust over your body. Maybe you have decided to dress how you like and believe that guys need to learn how to control their thoughts. To tell you the truth, some guys do control their thinking, but most guys find it extremely difficult. When your outfit leads them to lust, you can end up being the one who is hurt. Even "Christian" guys will try to get what they want. Just because a guy says he is a Christian doesn't mean that he is. The guys who are truly seeking the Lord will be turned off by a woman who wears revealing clothes.

In my case, the guys at school were drooling, but the guys at my church were turning their heads in the other direction. God made guys visual, and Christian or not, it is hard for them to avoid lustful thoughts. God created women too—to encourage guys, not to tempt or entice them. You don't want to attract a guy who has no respect for you. What you really want is to attract a wise man, but if you try to do it with the way you look or dress, you will never succeed! A wise man looks for beauty hidden beneath the skin.

The way you present yourself is captivating to the man's eyes. Do you want that to be negative or positive?

So I encourage you, the next time you are standing in front of the mirror, ask yourself, "Who am I trying to impress? Is my shirt cut too low? Is this skirt too short? Can I see through this material?" If you don't know the answer, go ask your mom or dad. Most likely, either one will be honest. When my sister bought a basically backless shirt, one with only a few strings holding it together, my dad, startled by this piece of fabric, asked, "Where's the rest of the shirt? Did it fall off before you reached home?" He said she shouldn't wear it. I actually ended up wearing it once, and that was a big mistake. If I would have listened to my father, I would have avoided a lot of pain. The way you present yourself is captivating to the man's eyes. Do you want that to be negative or positive? Do you want guys lusting over your body or loving your heart? It is up to you.

Time Well Spent?

How much time do you spend in front of the mirror? It is so easy for women to spend hour upon hour trying to perfect every single flaw. If you think you know someone who has perfect skin, they will not agree. Even models don't have perfect skin; their pictures are airbrushed to look flawless. Whenever I face a mirror, lies always seem to follow. I believe that Satan joins in while we consider our appearance. Every woman sizes up her own face and body shape. We look in the mirror and if Satan is there, we might think: "I am so ugly! I have all these blemishes. My lips are too small (or too big). My ears are deformed." Then after rehearsing all the flaws on our face, we move on to our body shape with: "I am too fat. My thighs are huge. My stomach is disgusting. My hips are wide." When Satan comes with me to the mirror, I end up saying all these things aloud. Every girl, whether she admits it or not, struggles with her appearance.

Look at the world's example of the perfect woman—she is everywhere: in the movies, on television, and on billboards; she is described in songs, she models for all the advertisements, and she is in every magazine. This "perfect woman" is skinny, fit, and has no body fat anywhere; her skin is flawless, she has beautiful, healthy hair with no dead ends, she has the most captivating features, turns the head of every man, and she is confident. This is the model woman the media tells us we are supposed to be. This is the woman that Satan says we have to look like; and that if we don't, we will be miserable. This image is what Satan and the world screams at us every time we look in the mirror. If you remember anything that I say, above all else, remember this one thing: The perfect woman is unrealistic! There is no such thing as a perfect woman. You can spend all the money in the world, try everything imaginable, and you will live your whole life always falling short of perfection. It is sad because even movie stars fall into the trap of needing to be perfect. We look at movie stars, thinking they are the ones with the perfect bodies when they don't even think that about themselves. Not one woman is perfect.

I believe the biggest lie going around in today's culture is that average women are too fat. More and more women give in to this lie and then run to the extreme of not eating. This is unhealthy and deadly, but in some way or another, we all struggle with it. During one of my years in high school, a few girls struggled with anorexia. The next year, four more girls fell into that trap and all lost an exorbitant amount of weight. They might have thought they looked good, but in actuality, they looked very unhealthy and sick. Their bodies became their idols; they were consumed with how they looked and felt about their bodies. This is one of the enemy's biggest traps for women of all ages. He will do anything to get our focus off the Lord; and giving in to the temptation of anorexia or bulimia will immediately remove a person's focus from God.

One of my closest friends had struggled with anorexia before I knew her. When she showed me pictures, I didn't even recognize her. She looked like two different people. She ended up in the hospital praying for her life, but by the grace of God, she still lives. She had told me that when someone struggles with an eating disorder, they look in the mirror and see themselves fat no matter how skinny they are. These are lies straight from the pit, she believed them, and they almost took her life.

Surgery won't fix anything. I hear that when you get it done once, it is extremely hard to stop. It is addicting and expensive. Lip injections, face-lifts, liposuction, all these things will never remain intact. The law of gravity is a law, and age takes its toll on everything. Everyone wants something else. If you have straight hair, you want curly hair; if you have curly hair, you want straight hair; if you have brown hair, you want blonde or red hair (or the other way around); if you are heavy, you want to be thinner; if you are thin, you still want to be thinner; if you are short, you want to be tall; if you are tall, you want to be short. I could go on forever, and I know you understand what I am saying. We are never satisfied with the way we look.

I have struggled with everything I have listed. I struggle with being thinner, being prettier, having perfect hair and skin, but I don't *dwell* on these things. I put them straight out of mind because I know they are just lies of the enemy. If I dwelt on these things and then started to pursue them, my life would only spiral downward. We all want to be like this fictional "perfect woman," but the more you desire to be like her, the sooner you will be let down. If you are so concerned with your outward appearance and do everything you can to make it perfect, you will attract guys who are only interested in your appearance. I would never want a guy interested in only my appearance because that would result in a life dedicated to maintaining my physical features. I would only be let down time after time, because I am not perfect, and that guy would take off as soon as he found someone prettier. We need to keep our minds pure from the world's deceptions. It's like keeping a clean house:

> *"When an unclean spirit goes out of a man, he goes through dry places, seeking rest, and finds none. Then he says, 'I will return to my house from which I came.' And when he comes, he finds it empty, swept, and put in order. Then he goes and takes with him seven other spirits more wicked than himself, and they enter and dwell there; and the last state of that man is worse than the first."*
>
> —Matthew 12:43–45

Just like this man, we need to sweep our minds clean and get rid of all the lies that fill our heads. These lies are like the demons in this story. They possess our minds and cause us to take destructive actions against ourselves. Listen, we need to take every thought captive and filter all the lies out. Ask God to fill you with His Holy Spirit and empower you to stand firm against these lies. But it is important once you clean your mind out of these lies, that you do not leave it empty. Just like the man who left his body empty, these lies will come seven times harder and stronger than they did before. Because truth blots out lies, fill your mind with God's encouraging words. Write verses on 3x5 cards and tape them everywhere. Tape verses like Psalm 139:14 or 1 Peter 3:3–4 on your mirror. Then, when you look into the mirror, you will be filled with God's love for you instead of Satan's lies. Fill your mind with the truth so you will be able to discern lies when you hear them.

Real Lasting Beauty

Earlier in this chapter I talked about how important it is that you dress modestly and how spending too much time in front of the mirror can end in a life of disappointment. I am not saying that you should never look in the mirror and that you should wear old, gross clothing. It is important to look presentable. I always desire to look nice and have good hygiene. That is important, but too much time taken on your appearance is dangerous. If you want real lasting beauty, spend more time looking into the mirror of God's Word. This is what He says:

> *Do not let your adornment be merely outward—arranging the hair, wearing gold, or putting on fine apparel—rather let it be the hidden person of the heart, with the incorruptible beauty of a gentle and quiet spirit, which is very precious in the sight of God.*
>
> —1 Peter 3:3–4

True beauty lies hidden within one's heart and character; it develops when spending time with God. I love the ending of this verse, which says, *"... is very precious in the sight of God."* Your inward beauty is so precious to God, your Father. I think that is such a wonderful quality of God—that He loves us and tells us how precious we are to Him. If a boy ever found interest in me or wrote me a letter confessing that interest, my heart would beat wildly fast and butterflies would flutter through my whole body. Have you ever felt those intense emotions and excitement knowing that someone adores you? That is how God, my Prince, makes me feel through His Word, and the above verse is just one example. My heart beats so fast when I read His Word and it says that I am so precious in His sight. So many girls sacrifice their whole heart and integrity looking for this kind of affection from the opposite sex; but you don't have to look very far—the affection and love you are searching for and desiring is right in front of you. You are extremely precious in God's sight; is your heart beating for Him?

God's light will radiate beauty throughout your life.

In his book, *Be Hopeful*, Warren Wiersbe writes, "Glamour is artificial and external; true beauty is real and internal. Glamour is something a person can put on and take off, but true beauty is always present. Glamour is corruptible; it decays and fades. True beauty from the heart grows more wonderful as the years pass. A Christian woman who cultivates the beauty of the inner person will not have to depend on cheap externals. God is concerned about values, not prices."[10]

God's light will radiate beauty throughout your life. I heard a pastor say that a wise man looks for a woman who possesses a natural radiance rather than a glow from a bottle. Girls, you want to attract a man first to who you are, and then your outward appearance will be a bonus. Your inner beauty is the key element. You are a beautiful woman; God created you just the way you are, and He wants to bless you with an amazing man as your husband. God also knows that the one He has for you will love you for who you are. He will cherish you, respect you, and unconditionally love you. When you spend time with God—reading, praying, and worshiping Him—your beauty will become incorruptible. The beauty that the world tells us to possess will fade with time, but the beauty that God asks us to pursue is imperishable. How would you like to possess that kind of beauty, a beauty that won't age or give in to the law of gravity? Ruth had this kind of beauty.

The Bible never says what Ruth looked like. We don't know if she was extremely beautiful, or if she was even physically attractive at all. We know Ruth was from Moab, a land of idol worship. She was a widow and she was poor, but she committed to staying with Naomi, her mother-in-law, and she committed her life to God. Ruth's mother-in-law pleaded with her to return to her own mother's home. Consider Ruth's reply:

> *Entreat me not to leave you, or to turn back from following after you; for wherever you go, I will go; and wherever you lodge, I will lodge; your people shall be my people, and your God, my God. Where you die, I will die, and there will I be buried. The Lord do so to me, and more also, if anything but death parts you and me.*
>
> —Ruth 1:16–17

This statement shows us Ruth's heart. *Halley's Bible Handbook* states, "She had a burst of devotion of superb beauty."[11] Ruth possessed rare and imperishable beauty beyond her years. We learn of her beauty from her actions, not from a description of her physical appearance. One of the greatest compliments a person can give is that the beauty of Jesus is flowing throughout your life. Ruth had this beauty in her heart, and it reflected in her life.

When Ruth returned to Naomi's homeland, she ventured into Boaz's field. Ruth had recently lost her husband, and God was leading her into a remarkable life. This is what catches my attention—when Boaz sees Ruth in his field, he goes to her, blesses her, and encourages her. Then he asks someone else who she is. He was interested in her, so he asked, but when he found her name was Ruth, he realized he already knew much about her. He had heard of her devotion to her mother-in-law, the love that poured from her life and her character. Boaz could have been interested in Ruth even before he met her because of the reputation she had in Bethlehem. When Boaz finally saw that this woman in his field was Ruth, his heart must have leapt. Could you imagine catching the interest of a man who knew only about your character? I would rather have someone who doesn't know me be interested in me because of my character than someone who was interested in me because of my looks. One is incorruptible; the other is corruptible. Boaz took Ruth for his wife and they became the great-great grandparents of David. Jesus came from the line of David—and Ruth and Boaz were also part of the lineage of Jesus. God's plan is so amazing. Wisdom teaches that *"charm is deceitful and beauty is passing, but a woman who fears the LORD, she shall be praised"* (Proverbs 31:30).

I am so thankful that I didn't marry my husband based primarily on his physical appearance (that was a bonus). If you marry someone based on looks, what are you going to say during a huge trial, "Well, at least you are handsome. I know we can't pay our mortgage, but I am so glad you are good looking"? You don't want a guy to say that about you either. Possessing an incorruptible beauty is the most attractive attribute any woman could have. Having the fear of the Lord brings praise to your name not because of who you are, but because of who Christ is. So many people will be attracted to the Lord in you, and He will use you and take you to great heights in your life. Can you imagine having a heart for God that causes the people around you to praise Him? Spend time in the presence of the Lord and you will begin to possess a beauty that is deeper than the surface of your skin.

I want to tell you about two girls I went to school with. Everyone liked both of these girls. All the guys liked one of the girls because she was beautiful. They would call her, want to hang out with her, and they all wanted to date her. She would spend a little extra time on the way she looked, but many guys found that there wasn't much under the surface. The other girl possessed a radiance and beauty that was deeper than her skin. She wasn't the most beautiful girl at school, but everyone wanted to hang out with her. Her beauty was contagious and people were attracted to the Lord in her, and they all just wanted to be her friend. She was such an example to me, because when you got underneath the surface, there still was so much more life in her. She had (and still has) the whole package. She was devoted to the Lord and she spent the extra time pursuing Him, not on the way she looked.

There are qualities to look for in a spouse, but don't forget that someone is looking for these great qualities in you too. Do you possess an incorruptible beauty? Are you attracting guys to your body by the way you dress and by the time you spend in front of the mirror? Or are you attracting guys to your heart, your character, your integrity, and your love for the Lord? Spend the extra time with God; He is waiting and desiring to bless you and mold you into a more beautiful woman, both inside and out.

chapter nine

Free from the Bondage of Sin

Jesus answered them, "Most assuredly, I say to you, whoever commits sin is a slave of sin."

—John 8:34

When we give in to sin we become its slave, and that is when breaking free becomes much more difficult; in fact it can sometimes seem impossible. No matter how deep into sin we are, it is possible to become free. I don't know what you are going through, I don't know the pressures that you are facing, and I don't know the temptations that you are struggling with, but I do know what it is to go through tough times. I know what it is like to struggle with temptations, and I know what it is like to give in to pressure. We are all faced with these situations, sometimes every day. Satan's goal is to get your focus off Jesus, and he will use the world and its full potential to lure you into his deadly trap. Beware if you think that you will never give in to temptation. We are all a huge target for Satan. First Corinthians 10:12 warns, *"Therefore let him who thinks he stands take heed lest he fall."* Sadly, I know too many guys and girls who are doing the very things they had stood so strongly against. It is so easy to let your guard down for one second and be sucked into Satan's trap. It happened to me and it can happen to you too.

For my whole life, I had held strong to my convictions. I had never stolen anything, I would never dare say a curse word, and I made a commitment that my very first kiss was going to be on my wedding day. I wouldn't even think about drinking alcohol or smoking. All these were no-brainers for me because I was committed to never doing them. I wasn't puffed up about it; I just knew that I would never give in. So with each commitment, with each promise, and with each decision against the world's pleasures, I became a growing target for Satan. He was planning, devising, and watching. He was waiting for the perfect moment, when I was at my weakest, and then he attacked with all his might … and he succeeded.

I was sixteen when I was first offered alcohol, and by that

time, I knew others who drank. I remember the boy who sat next to me in a few of my high school classes. He had just moved to California and didn't have many friends, but he was so happy all the time. He always smiled and we would talk a lot in class (only when we had free time, of course). But then I noticed that something was happening to him. He didn't smile any more. His face seemed pale and his eyes were red. He had dark circles under his eyes and he slurred his words when he spoke. I finally asked him what was going on. His new girlfriend had gotten him to start drinking. My heart sank. When I asked him if he really enjoyed drinking, he said he did it because he didn't want to lose his girlfriend. I couldn't believe it. Here was this smart guy with a lot going for him and now firsthand I was watching his life disintegrate. I told him every day that he needed to stop drinking. I told him I never had drunk alcohol and how I never would because it destroys lives. He wouldn't listen; I don't know how his life turned out.

My point of sharing this story is that I was the one who scolded him for drinking almost every day. I had also watched alcohol ruin my grandfather's life and the life of a man who was paralyzed after being hit by a drunk driver. I knew of a girl killed in a car accident; even though she was not driving and was the only one in the car who hadn't been drinking, she was the only one killed in the accident. I don't think my parents ever had a drink of alcohol. They taught us children the repercussions of drinking, and I knew better than to give in to its pressure. I knew its consequences and I was completely against it. So why was I such a huge target? I had never been tempted to drink and Satan knew that. He also knew that if he cornered me at the right moment, I would give in to this temptation. I had no idea what I was about to face.

The night I was offered alcohol I had no desire to drink and explained, "No. I don't want any." But the girl who was offering it to me kept pressuring, "Listen, it doesn't matter what other people think." So I answered, "I really don't care what other people think, so I don't want any." She kept repeating, "Don't care what other people will think of you." I was so frustrated with her because I had made up my mind, and other peoples' opinions had nothing to do with my decision. We kept going back and forth for about half an hour, when finally she put an open bottle in my lap and said, "Just hold on to this." I didn't have to do anything. I could have just held on and not taken a sip; I could have really said no and easily handed it back, but I didn't. I looked at it; my heart was pounding, and then I took just a sip. I gave in to Satan's plan. I compromised. All of my convictions went flying out the window as I took my first step in to that sin.

I have regretted that stupid decision my entire life because it didn't stop that night. I actually enjoyed it. Satan makes sin so desirable. If it wasn't, no one would be tempted to give in. Think of coffee—it smells so good and looks amazingly refreshing; however, when you first drink black coffee, it is disgusting (it tastes like dirt). It never tastes as good as it smells. Then you add a little bit of sugar and cream, and before you know it, you are addicted. Why in your right mind would you want to do something that doesn't appear exciting or fun? I enjoyed the temporary pleasure without thinking about the consequences and eventually became a slave to it. A few of my so-called friends actually applauded my actions and wanted to throw me a party. They explained that I had finally gotten off my throne of innocence and now I could hang out with them and do the things they did. For almost two years, I was unable to stop drinking alcohol.

Every morning after a night of drinking, guilt, regret, and

pain would overflow my entire body. Each time, I would cry out to the Lord, on my knees, weeping. I didn't want to do this. I was hurting my Father, I was hurting my real friends, and I was hurting my family. I became the epitome of a hypocrite. I still went to church trying to get my life right with the Lord. I wanted to walk with Him so badly, but I wasn't able to juggle both lives. I was trying to make two totally different lives work. I was trying to dwell in the dark while walking in the light, and it was destroying me. Guilt flooded me every moment I was at church; conviction nearly ate me alive every time I fed my flesh. No matter what I did, I only felt guilt or conviction—never joy. I had to justify my actions. Satan would tell me that drinking was okay, that I wasn't hurting anyone, and that I was just having a little bit of fun; but I was destroying my life, and causing pain to the lives of others, and all I wanted to do was die. I didn't want to exist. I thought that maybe if I died I would stop hurting everyone and then I would stop sinning.

Sin leaves deep scars on your life and on others' lives. If you think that your choices won't affect other people, you are wrong.

That was exactly where Satan wanted me. He wanted me to take my life; he wanted me to die. He was overjoyed at my decaying state. Satan rejoices over your pain and sorrow. He rejoices because he hates God and he hates everyone who loves God. God offers life, everlasting life, while Satan offers death, pain, destruction, and eternal damnation. I was pleasing Satan. I would ask God for forgiveness for what I had done the night before, and then my day would be okay; but by the time the weekend came along, I would drink again. Over and over, this cycle continued with me asking God for forgiveness, saying I was going to stop, and then drinking again. I was living a life of remorse, not repentance, and it became impossible for me to stop.

When you choose sin, the consequences will be greater than you can imagine. Sin leaves deep scars on your life and on others' lives. If you think that your choices won't affect other people, you are wrong. Your sin affects everyone around you and it can deeply affect people you don't even know. I had so many friends who, I later found out, had been praying for me that whole time. I had other friends who tried to talk to me and begged me to stop destroying my life. I had friends who cared so much about me that they would start crying while they talked to me. But my heart had turned selfishly hard and bitter. I pushed those friends aside. I didn't care about anyone but myself. Sin will do that. You won't care about all the people who are burdened for you. You won't care to listen to those who love you and only want the best for you. You won't care about the amount of pain others feel because of you. I only hurt the people who really loved me.

The friends I went drinking with weren't really my friends. They didn't care about me. If I was in trouble, they were nowhere to be found. The people who deeply loved and cared about me were always there, no matter what, and my actions were devastating them. I will never forget my dad's reaction when he found out about what I was doing. It tore him to pieces; he was overwhelmed with sorrow. There are only three times I saw my dad really cry and this was one of them. Seeing my dad's pain tore me up inside. When I saw my actions rip him to shreds, it brought me to my knees, and it was then I began to wonder how much more my Father in heaven must be hurting over me.

Jesus gave His life for me. He suffered and was beaten; His

flesh was torn to meat, He hung on a cross, and He died for me—and for you. He died that we might have life. My choices were causing Him pain. He was grieving over me. Every time I chose to sin, He would have to turn His face away. With every sip of alcohol and with every time I took His name in vain, nails were driven deeper into His hands and feet. I can't even comprehend the depth of His love for me, how every single moment He continued working in and through my life. No matter what I was doing against Him, He still was not done with me. He never gave up on me, and He has never and will never give up on you.

My parents pulled me out of public high school and began a home school program. After one semester at home, I was accepted into a Christian school. Also, there was a list of people I was forbidden to hang out with. When I didn't see those people every day at school any more, it was easier not to hang out with them. Still, I was a slave to my sin. No matter what I did, I couldn't get away from it. But God was working in spite of my situation. A Christian owned the surf shop where I was hired, my manager was a Christian, and almost all of my fellow employees were Christians. God flooded my life with godly friends who loved me and cared about me.

Still, Satan was pulling me down. At every turn, sin seemed more enticing. I managed to find myself hanging out with the people who said they were Christians but who, on the inside, were far from God. I hung out with the people who were just like me. Part of me wanted to hang out with those who were truly in love with God, but it was so hard because Satan had a hold on my life. I couldn't get away from the temptation. I tried to go to church more often; I tried to read my Bible more; I tried to pray more; and I started hanging out with the people who were truly in love with God, even if they didn't want to hang out with me.

None of that made me a better person. Despite all my efforts, I could not escape my desire to drink. I had hit bottom. I wanted to change. I didn't want to live in the dark any more. I didn't want to be a hypocrite; I didn't want to hang out with people who were the same as me. I wanted to dwell in the light, I wanted to be happy again, I wanted to change … but *I* couldn't.

Then God spoke to me. He looked at me with His tender eyes and softly spoke, "You are completely unable to change yourself. Only I can change you. Only I can give you rest. Only I can fill you with joy. You need to surrender and give everything up to Me. Only then will you see a change." God asked me for my broken heart and my destroyed life; in exchange He offered me a new heart and a new life. He asked for my ashes so He could give me beauty. I realized that I could never change myself; only God could change me. I couldn't believe He would even want to after my rebellion; and I couldn't believe that He desired to do more than just change me—He desired to save me. He sent His only Son to suffer and die on the cross for my sin. I was off partying and drinking and He was dying for those sins. My sins were the nails that held Him on the cross. He didn't have to give His life or shed His blood for me, but He did. He easily could have come down from the cross, but He didn't. I don't deserve to live. I am guilty of my sin and I deserve to die. *"For the wages of sin is death, but the gift of God is eternal life in Christ Jesus our Lord"* (Romans 6:23). He paid the debt for my sin so I wouldn't have to. At that moment, I fell to my knees weeping and gave it all up to Him. I surrendered to Him my whole self, and He has completely changed my entire life. I have not once had a desire to drink alcohol since.

If you are in bondage to sin, know that God is able to set you free. All sin is the same in God's eyes. There is no sin greater than another. Even if you are sleeping with your boyfriend, struggling with an eating disorder, doing drugs, getting drunk, living promiscuously, stealing, or swearing like a sailor, there is still hope for you. You can break free from the bondage of sin; however, know that nothing you attempt to do in your own strength will make you change. *"With men it is impossible, but not with God; for with God all things are possible"* (Mark 10:27). God desires so much to give you a new life; He wants to bless you more than you could know. He desires to give you rest and encourages, *"Come to Me, all you who labor and are heavy laden, and I will give you rest. Take My yoke upon you and learn from Me, for I am gentle and lowly in heart, and you will find rest for your souls. For My yoke is easy and My burden is light"* (Matthew 11:28–30). All you have to do is go to Him. He is waiting with His arms open wide. He has already taken your sin away; He did that on the cross, but you need to give your life to Him.

Picture your life as a single straight line. The beginning of the line is your birth and the end of the line is heaven, our goal. All you have to do is walk a straight path. Then temptation comes and you veer off the course—straying into loops and zigzags—and you find yourself very far from the simple path. What do you need to do to get back on the path toward heaven? Must you walk back the way you came? Do you need to change the way you are and hope you can return? Do you think you have gone so far that you will be lost eternally? No. Turn around one hundred and eighty degrees, Jesus is standing right there. But beware: Satan is also there to convince you it is hopeless, that you will never change. You might as well keep doing what you're doing. Satan will remind you that everyone makes mistakes, so it is okay if you do too. If these are your thoughts, then you are listening to Satan. God, on the other hand, truly desires to give you rest. He wants you to reign with Him for all eternity and promises beauty for ashes.

So, if you desire to have a new life, if you desire to break free from the bondage of sin and live a restful life with Christ, first you need to realize that you cannot do it on your own. You are completely unable to break free from your sin. Second, you need to tell your Father that you need Him. Third, you need to surrender to Christ. Pray something like this:

> *Father, I am a sinner and I have been hurting You. I am so sorry. Please forgive me for what I have done. I desire to change and I desire to stop, but I am unable to change on my own. I can't change myself. I need You to come and take over my life. Please come into my life again and change me. I surrender completely to You. Thank You for dying on the cross and giving Your life for me. I now surrender my life to You. I only want Your best.*

Realize that surrendering, like temptation, is continual. You may have to do it every five minutes. *"Therefore submit to God. Resist the devil and he will flee from you"* (James 4:7). This verse doesn't say "Resist the devil just once and he will flee from you forever." No, you must keep resisting sin and keep submitting to God. Every time you are faced with temptation, you need to surrender to God; every time the thought creeps into your head, you need to surrender; every time you wake up in the morning, you need to surrender. Satan is still there trying to make you fall, so you need to resist him and *keep* resisting him.

Too many of my friends have fallen away from the Lord. Some of the people who influenced me greatly for the Lord have now turned their backs on the truth they taught me. It is heartbreaking to watch my closest friends' lives crumble before my very eyes. The people I thought would never fall away from God have fallen away. I now know what it feels like to be on the other side of the equation. I understand the pain I put so many people through because now I am burdened by my friends' actions. I can't help but cry over my closest friends who are walking in darkness. I fall on my knees before the Lord for my friends. I know guys who were so committed to God, but now they are living with their girlfriends and getting drunk all the time. I know those who used to be worship leaders or high school ministry leaders who now either party all the time or are constantly high on drugs.

This is reality. Satan is out to destroy you, and he will do all he can to get you to compromise.

I remember getting into a huge fight with one of my best guy friends from high school. He said that if someone put a gun to his head and asked, "Do you love God?" he would not hesitate and say yes. He was certain that, if put to the test, he would confess and die for Christ; so he became angry when I questioned how he could know for sure. I argued that Peter had told Jesus that even if he had to die, he would never deny Him. But Peter denied Christ three times. We didn't stop fighting over this for almost half a year. He fell away from Christ; and later, I had a dream that I put a gun to his head, asking him if he would die for his belief in Christ, and he said no. It broke my heart to see that he wasn't living for Christ any more.

I even personally know a pastor who left the church, left his wife, and ran off with the secretary. This is reality. Satan is out to destroy you, and he will do all he can to get you to compromise.

You need to be aware that you are just as capable of falling as Peter was. Peter was certain he would never deny Christ, but he did. I was certain I would never drink, and I did. We are all human and we are all tempted. Resist the devil every day.

Part of resisting is strategy. Make sure you put your armor on every morning, and then keep it on!

> *Therefore take up the whole armor of God, that you may be able to withstand in the evil day, and having done all, to stand. Stand therefore, having girded your waist with truth, having put on the breastplate of righteousness, and having shod your feet with the preparation of the gospel of peace; above all, taking the shield of faith with which you will be able to quench all the fiery darts of the wicked one. And take the helmet of salvation, and the sword of the Spirit, which is the word of God; praying always with all prayer and supplication in the Spirit, being watchful to this end with all perseverance and supplication for all the saints.*
>
> —Ephesians 6:13–18

Girding your waist with truth means you understand the gospel and are able to explain it to others. You need to be able to defend what you believe to anyone who questions it. *"But sanctify the Lord God in your hearts, and always be ready to give a defense to everyone who asks you a reason for the hope that is in you, with meekness and fear"* (1 Peter 3:15). Once you realize only Jesus' blood can make you righteous before God, put on the *breastplate of righteousness. Equipping your feet with the gospel* means being able to tell others about the good news so you can share its message wherever you go—to school, to the grocery store, to work, or even to another country. Next, take up the *shield of faith*, and trust the Lord rather than your own thoughts and ideas. *"For we walk by faith, not by sight"* (2 Corinthians 5:7). Then, when the enemy directs fiery darts at you daily, the shield of faith resists them. Satan wants you to walk away from the Lord and asks, "Why believe in something you can't see?" However, you can confidently walk in faith knowing that you have seen God work in and through your life. Once you have given your life to the Lord, you have been saved. Putting on the *helmet of salvation* means knowing that you are saved and believing it, trusting that you will reign with the Lord for all eternity. Next, the sword is the *Word of God*. You need to read it and be fully prepared to use it against the enemy. Fill your mind with His Word so you can pierce all lies that will come your way. *"For the word of God is living and powerful, and sharper than any two-edged sword, piercing even to the division of soul and spirit, and of joints and marrow, and is a discerner of the thoughts and intents of the heart"* (Hebrews 4:12). Lastly, *pray always*. Doing these things daily enables you to resist temptation. But you must remember to do them *every day*.

> *I beseech you therefore, brethren, by the mercies of God, that you present your bodies a living sacrifice, holy, acceptable to God, which is your reasonable service. And do not be conformed to this world, but be transformed by the renewing of your mind, that you may prove what is that good and acceptable and perfect will of God.*
>
> —Romans 12:1–2

Do not conform to this world. God wants to use you in ways you cannot imagine. He has prepared a place for you in eternity. Choose every day to follow Christ. *"And God is able to make all grace abound toward you, that you, always having all sufficiency in all things, may have an abundance for every good work"* (2

Corinthians 9:8). *"Being confident of this very thing, that He who has begun a good work in you will complete it until the day of Jesus Christ"* (Philippians 1:5–7). *"That you may walk worthy of the Lord, fully pleasing Him, being fruitful in every good work and increasing in the knowledge of God"* (Colossians 1:10). He will finish that good work He started in you as He is doing with me every day.

If you have surrendered your life to Christ and have broken free from the bondage of sin, but you still feel guilt and condemnation, understand that is also from Satan. He will try as hard as he can to make you feel guilty and useless. But remember, *"there is therefore now no condemnation to those who are in Christ Jesus, who do not walk according to the flesh, but according to the Spirit"* (Romans 8:1). God has set you free, He has forgiven you of your sins, and He remembers them no more. *"As far as the east is from the west, so far has He removed our transgressions from us"* (Psalm 103:12). He has washed you white as snow with His blood. It is finished! Remember His promises, if you feel condemned or guilty, and know that these feelings come from Satan. Keep resisting him, *"Fight the good fight of faith, lay hold on eternal life"* (1 Timothy 6:12). Put on all your armor! I desire God to look at me and say, *"Well done, good and faithful servant ... Enter into the joy of your lord"* (Matthew 25:21). I also pray that you, dear friend, will desire to hear these words and will choose to live a life after God's own heart.

chapter ten

A Guy's Perspective

by Dan Leitz

"Behold, I send you out as sheep in the midst of wolves. Therefore be wise as serpents and harmless as doves."

—Matthew 10:16

When my wife asked me to write a section in her book on waiting for "the one," I thought it sounded like a good idea; however, the more I thought about it, the more the enemy tried to get me distracted with my past impure life. You see, I didn't wait for "the one," so it seems a little weird that a guy who didn't wait would contribute to a book on waiting. But as I have come to find out in my life as a Christian, I serve an amazing God who has forgiven me of all my past mistakes, and He sees them no more. I am seen through the blood of Jesus as pure and holy in the sight of God. My prayer is that you will truly take to heart what I tell you in this chapter and that it will help you reflect on who God is. Some people can learn from others' mistakes, but unfortunately, other people choose to learn by experiencing the downfalls and perils of making these mistakes themselves. I implore you to learn from my mistakes.

I was raised in a Christian home, maybe similar to yours. Like me, there might be a few of you who don't really buy into the whole "Christian" thing. Maybe your mom gave you this book to read because she is concerned. Maybe you saw this book on a shelf and were expecting a step-by-step, how-to book on relationships, like one of those magazines you see at the checkout counter at your local grocery store. Whatever the reason, I know that the Lord has you reading this for a very specific reason.

You might have already asked yourself (like I did), "Why is a guy even writing in a book that is intended for girls? What would he know about girls' desires, passions, feelings, thoughts, and other intricacies which make them unique?" Well … I know a little. I grew up as the only boy among three girls. The emotions in our home ran very high and the hand-me-downs just didn't seem to fit me. It was just my dad and I trying to survive in an emotionally volatile household. But on a more serious note, the whole reason for me writing this chapter is to give all you ladies a look into what is going on in "his" mind, and since I am a "him" I *do* know what I am talking about.

Wants versus Needs

You've all probably heard it said that girls mature faster than boys. Well, as a "boy," I emphatically agree. Now don't get all prideful right here and think that because you're a girl you are fully mature. I said that girls mature *faster*, not that all of you have reached full maturity by the magical age of eighteen. I'm twenty-seven years old and realize that I still have a way to go. I look back to things I did just last week and think, "that was so immature." Believe me, no matter how old we get we will always have episodes of immaturity. yay. good!

Over the past few years, I have had the privilege of being a high school teacher and have seen firsthand that (for the most part) girls mature much faster than guys. It is eye opening being on the outside looking in. I began teaching at twenty-three, so I could still vividly remember my own high school experience. I watched some of my guy students and asked myself, "Is that the way I was? Did I act like that?" Sadly, the answer in most cases is yes. At the time, it probably all seemed perfectly reasonable, but now I get embarrassed even thinking about the bonehead moves I pulled. Unfortunately, the only remedy for those dumb high school moves is time. Why? Well, it took time for the Lord to show me (actually it took me time to start listening). The things I wanted in high school were not the things I wanted in college. The things I wanted when I started college were not the things I wanted when I finished college, and the things I wanted when I finished college are not the things I *need* now. Do you see how things change? They changed from wants to needs and from my desires to His desires.

Think about it. You have almost certainly experienced the same thing. Look back to just last year; there were probably several things you wanted so bad, but now could really care less about. The guy you may have been so infatuated with before now causes you to question your own sanity. There was that piece of clothing (or "accessory") you would have given anything for, only to realize it went out of style the second it came out and that everyone else had it too. Our wants, desires, feelings, and dreams change so drastically over the years that very few people have their lives figured out in high school. But you might think, "I do know what I want in life." Well, so did I, and so did most people. Just ask your parents, neighbors, friends' parents, pastor, grandparent, teacher, professor, mayor, or the president himself, and they will most likely tell you they thought they had life figured out by the ripe old age of seventeen, but they were wrong.

"Life" Figured Out

I went to church because my parents made me. If I ever missed going to church I felt like I had done something horribly wrong and that God was mad at me. For me, church was a ritual, not a relationship. So, as a Christian by name and with a heart that was far from the Lord, I became a walking contradiction—professing Christ with my lips and doing the exact opposite with my actions.

By the age of nineteen, *I* had my life planned. I had dated my high school sweetheart for two and a half years. She was (at that time) "the one." I had a good-paying, full-time job at an upscale grocery store, was going to college to get my degrees, and was living with my parents to save money for "the ring." My plan was to finish school, buy the ring, get married to "the one," buy a house, have a few kids, go to work, catch a ball game with the family every now and then, go to church on Sundays, mow the lawn on the weekend, do other dad things, and live happily ever after. This was, after all, what *I* wanted. This verse will help you understand what happened next. Isaiah 55:8 explains, *"'For My thoughts are not your thoughts, nor are your ways My ways,' says the LORD."*

As you can probably figure out, my way wasn't in the cards. It turned out my sweetheart wasn't as sweet as I thought. We broke up and life as I knew it fell apart. I won't bore you with all of the details, but I will tell you it was bad. At that point, my fragile brain was not ready to handle such trauma. I had never thought of the "what if things don't work out" scenario. It was like a wicked snowball effect my mind took to the extreme. I found myself thinking of my future as a lonely, unhappy, fat, balding, middle-aged man who lost everything when he was nineteen. It was truly a sad day. This was my life—my future—and it was ruined. I had put all my eggs into that one basket and the bottom fell out. My plans were broken on the floor, over easy. I thought I had life figured out, but what I didn't figure was that God had a plan for my life, and He wasn't about to let me ruin it. Jeremiah 29:11 says it best: *"For I know the thoughts that I think toward you, says the LORD, thoughts of peace and not of evil, to give you a future and a hope."*

All the while I was living in this sinful relationship, not serving the Lord, and I had the nerve to question God when it fell apart. He took it away from me, and I had the guts to say, "How could God ...?" At the time, I could only see my bleak situation.

I did not, and do not, have the unique perspective that only God has—the ability to see the end. What I know now, I wish I had known then. It's like Paul, when he was writing to the Romans, was writing to me. Romans 8:28 reads, *"And we know that all things work together for good to those who love God, to those who are the called according to His purpose."* After a few days of soul searching, I realized that God was protecting me. He did not take the relationship away from me any more than I gave it away by living in a constant state of sin. Who was I serving anyway? I went to church and would follow that up by doing things with my girlfriend that broke the Lord's heart. I realize now that every second of that relationship I was hammering those nails deeper and deeper into the hands of Jesus. I came to understand that as we go through life, we don't have it all figured out. Not only that, but we never will. If we did, we wouldn't need the Lord.

The Non-Christian Christian

After a number of years of interacting with girls, I have noticed they have certain things in common. It seems that most girls want a guy to sweep them off their feet, they want to get married, and they want to have kids, in that order—even if they say they don't. I knew this about girls and I preyed upon it. In name, I was a Christian. I portrayed myself as a Christian. I played the game. But inside I was far from the Lord. I said whatever I needed in order to get what I wanted. Sometimes I meant it, sometimes I didn't. I played the game and broke some hearts. It's not something I say with pride, but with great remorse. And I give you this warning: there are a lot of guys out there who do the same thing.

What exactly is a non-Christian Christian? Here is what they look like. They go to church and your youth group, and they say all the right things. They are nice and respectful to you, your parents, and their parents. They bring their Bible to church and even open it up during the study. They dress normal and shower regularly and sometimes they even smell nice. But here is the kicker: You have no idea what is going on inside their heads—there is a lot more. These guys will get you to give away your heart by saying everything you want to hear and then drop you once they have met the challenge.

> *What exactly is a non-Christian Christian? ... These guys will get you to give away your heart by saying everything you want to hear and then drop you once they have met the challenge.*

I am not by any means saying that any guy who looks like he has a relationship with Jesus is just putting up a front. What I am saying is there are many guys who do, and that is why you have to be careful. Matthew 10:16 warns us of people like this: *"Behold, I send you out as sheep in the midst of wolves. Therefore be wise as serpents and harmless as doves."* Not every guy in your church is a wolf. In fact, some of these guys might even have the best of intentions, but they lack discipline. Ladies, you need to be "as wise as serpents." It is up to you to check it out, and make sure the walk matches the talk. It does no good to say, "Well, he seems like a nice guy." What does that even mean? Looks can be deceiving. I looked the part, but there was nothing to it.

I have seen sweet Christian high school girls hanging out with guys I know are not walking with the Lord. When I have asked them, "Why are you hanging out with him?" "Is he a Christian?" in most cases, the girl will make excuses for the guy. They will say something like, "Well, he goes to church," or "He said he would come to church with me." Going to church doesn't make you a Christian any more than going to a garage makes you a car. Don't assume because you see a guy at church that he is walking with the Lord. Anyone can proclaim to be a Christian. Not everyone can walk the walk. Think about this recent poll conducted by *U.S. News and World Report*. Over 84 percent of U.S. citizens say they are Christians.[12] Eighty-four percent! I find that hard to believe. If even 50 percent were actually walking with the Lord, this country would not be the way it is. I had everyone believing that I was walking with the Lord in high school, but I was far from Him. In fact, I had not even made a profession of faith. I had never asked Jesus to come into my heart and be the center of my life. Was I a Christian? I don't think so.

It takes only a little time and effort to find out if someone is who he says he is. However, it also takes the right mind-set. When you really like a guy, it will be easy for you to find good things about him, and when you are looking for the good in someone you can usually find it. The phrase "blinded by love" implies that no matter how bad or gross a person is, the infatuated person sees it all as adorable, sweet, and cute. The right mind-set would lead you to ask other people about him, like your youth pastor or another adult who has a perspective outside of your swooning brain. I know why I never asked people outside of myself about a girl I liked. It was because I knew they would not support my decision.

You need to be honest and ask yourself, "Is this guy going to bring me closer to the Lord or take me away from Him?" If he will draw you away from Lord, then your relationship should end. Sadly, many people will sacrifice their own relationship with the Lord for missionary dating. These people believe that a dating pool filled with non-Christians is their mission field. Bad idea! In a more detailed summary, this is dating a guy or girl who does not have a relationship with the Lord; these guys or girls believe that somehow, through their relationship, he or she will get saved. If you are one of those people, I pray that you would stop because the behavior is very unbiblical. In 2 Corinthians 6:14, Paul says, *"Do not be unequally yoked together with unbelievers. For what fellowship has righteousness with lawlessness? And what communion has light with darkness?"* That is where the argument should end, but if you need to see an example, just find someone in your church who is married to a non-Christian and ask him or her how well it works.

Finally, I have one last point on the subject before I completely beat this horse to death. The Bible speaks of fruits. If you don't see any fruit in a person's life, chances are he is not walking with the Lord. But you also have to be very wise when it comes to looking for fruit. Jesus said in Matthew 7:17, *"Even so, every good tree bears good fruit, but a bad tree bears bad fruit."* There is such a thing as bad fruit. Look for it; seek it out. If it's bad fruit, leave it alone. If it's good fruit, pray about it. And follow my handy-dandy guide to dating.

My Step-by-Step Instructions for Dating

Step one: If you think that the Lord might be in it, search the Scriptures, pray about it, and wait. (If he *is* the one that God has for you, he's not going anywhere.)

Step two: If you still feel that the Lord is in it, search the Scriptures, pray about it, and wait.

Step three: If you still feel that the Lord is in it, search the Scriptures, pray about it, and wait some more.

Step four: If you still have not received an answer, repeat steps 1–3 until you do. Either way, for or against, the Lord *will* answer you. Remember, *no* is an answer.

I Have a Feeling ...

Whenever I ask someone how it is they know the Lord is in their relationship, they say a wide variety of things. Many are poor measurements when it comes to knowing if the Lord is truly in it. For example: "It just feels right ..." Here is the problem with "It just *feels* right," which quickly translates to "I *feel* like the Lord is in it," and let's not forget the famous, "I have never *felt* this way before, so it must be the Lord." What is the common theme? Give up? It's feelings. You know, the butterflies in your stomach, heartbeat racing, flood of emotion that you get when you are hanging out with the person you have liked for so long. It's the pit-of-your-stomach excitement you have when you find out that the guy you like has feelings for you. While these feelings are normal, they are not a good test to determine if the Lord is the author of what you are doing. Our feelings are constantly changing. You may even feel all gushy about a few different guys.

Jeremiah 17:9 should help put your feelings to rest: *"The heart is deceitful above all things, and desperately wicked; who can know it?"* If my heart/feelings and your heart/feelings are deceitful and desperately wicked, why would we listen to or trust them? I wouldn't. But then again, I have trusted my feelings before; we all have. The Lord tells us to test these feelings by the Word of God. First Thessalonians 5:21 says, *"Test all things; hold fast what is good."* If we don't, we are placing our feelings above God and we are subjecting ourselves to heartbreak. Worst of all our relationship with the Lord becomes completely one-sided.

The Lord wants to be involved in our lives, but too many times we shut Him out and replace God with only feelings. Let me conclude by saying this: The Lord gave us feelings as a gift, and He can use them for His good pleasure. Feelings are not wrong or bad; they are simply poor measurements to determine if God is really calling you to a relationship. Sometimes I get overwhelming feelings when I am worshiping God. The Holy Spirit washes over me and I feel close to God. I can test that feeling by the Scriptures and find examples all over the Bible of people having amazing feelings associated with the worship of God. I have tested and proved that those feelings are biblical. What we don't want is to base decisions on feelings that are random or ones we haven't tested by Scripture.

I had an experience in this. I really liked a girl while I was in college. She was beautiful, funny, smart, and above all a Christian. I thought I had hit the jackpot. We went out on a date that was so fun I could hardly believe it. It was the feeling that gave me butterflies in my stomach, made me dance when no one was looking, and let out a huge *yesss!* in front of my roommate for no reason. It was awesome. The only problem was that I never had any sort of confirmation from the Lord about going forward with the relationship. Nothing! I could see where I wanted to go, but I couldn't go there. It was like looking at something you want so badly, but through an impenetrable glass door. I couldn't understand what was going on. Everything seemed so perfect. But the Holy Spirit reminded me of the time I prayed for Him to keep me from anything and everything that was not His will for my life. It had nothing to do with her. It was that God had a different plan for me.

I think back to that time and wonder where I would be today if I had gone against the Lord's will and begun a relationship with that girl. Where would she be today? Would I have met my wife? Would I be writing this book right now? Would I even be walking with the Lord? The mere thought scares me. You see, every decision you make can drastically affect your future. Yes, the Lord does forgive, but there are consequences for our actions.

The Trap of "The One"

As a high school teacher, I have talked with so many girls who, by the age of seventeen, actually believe that their boyfriend is the one. I had two "the one's" before I met my wife at the age of twenty-five. This leads me to the conclusion that *the one* is a very ambiguous term. So many girls fall into what I call, "the trap of the one." *The one*, it's like these two words carry some mystifying power that makes people lose all common sense, and brain function drops off the chart. These two, three-letter words have the power to make the smartest people act stupid. Please don't misunderstand what I am trying to say here. I have seen high school sweethearts get married and have kids and live great Christian lives. It is not unheard of for this to happen; however, in my experience, it is not the norm.

Why is it that we feel a sense of urgency when it comes to getting married? I think most people fail to realize (as I did) that we will spend the majority of our life married. But we live in such a "got-to-have-it-now" society that whenever we see something, we want it now! The world says, "If it feels good, do it!" In the grand scheme of things, our society has put out the unstated rule that you should be married by the age of twenty-five, or at the latest, thirty. If not, it's pretty much over for you. The life that you have always dreamed of has passed you by. I bought into that lie too, but I have two friends that got married a few years back who were both were in their thirties. There is no one in the world that could tell them they waited too long or that love had passed them by. In fact, I believe that had they jumped the gun and not waited for the best that God had for them, they would not have the blessings they have now. Ladies, please understand that the Lord wants only the best for you. I have seen this promise firsthand. Don't get ripped off by the enemy and settle for less than God's best.

> *The one, it's like these two words carry some mystifying power that makes people lose all common sense, and brain function drops off the chart.*

Fuel on the Fire

God has created us with an innate desire for the opposite sex. Guys usually develop this attraction in the teen years. So, it is natural for guys to be attracted to girls; however, it is partly the girl's responsibility to make sure she is not throwing jet fuel on an already stoked fire.

If you haven't figured it out by now, guys are highly visual. Why do you think girls' clothing is designed the way it is? Low-cut this, see-through that, and clothes that seem to be painted on. These are designed to be attractive to the opposite sex. To this day, even being married, I have to make a conscious decision to look away from those things. If I don't, my mind will go to places that I don't want it to go. The hard thing to grasp is that I even have to do this at church. Now please understand that I am not some sick pervert, I am simply telling you that our hearts are perverted from birth. We, as Christians, need the Holy Spirit's help to keep our minds in check.

As I said previously, I was a high school teacher. Fortunately, it was at a Christian school where they had uniforms. However, I also helped with the Wednesday night high school study at the church. To be honest, it was more of a fashion show than a Bible study. Students would come just to see what everyone else looked like without a uniform. It was a giant stumble/flesh fest. I would watch guys undressing girls with their minds, and these were the so-called Christians. Ladies, remember, just because a guy goes to church, that doesn't make him a Christian. The clothes you wear say a lot about who you are. They could be true or they could be false. Either way you are not wearing a sign on your clothes saying, "The way I dress does not reflect who I am on the inside." You need to be aware of the fact that people judge a book by its cover all the time. Your clothes are the cover of your book. What does it say about who you are on the inside? Does it say, "I am looking for attention"? Or do you go unnoticed by the guys. Believe me the guy who only notices you for what you are wearing is the guy you want to stay away from, no matter how cute he is.

Waiting

As I alluded to earlier, I did not wait for the one God had for me. I did have sex before marriage; and let me tell you one thing: I regret it every day. Not to say that I live in guilt and shame every day, but that I really wish I had made different decisions. Think of how I felt when my wife told me before we got married that she had waited for me. The only thing I could say was, "Thank you." It hurt me, and I could only imagine what it felt like for her. I do know that I have been forgiven and that the Lord remembers it no more. The only problem is that I have a harder time forgetting. Our brains are like a computer hard drive that has no delete button. Every image, every thought, every word we have ever said is stored there. It is the enemy's greatest tool. He simply reminds us of our past failures and uses them against us. He tries to show us how dirty and disgusting we are; he'll exploit our sin. As for me, I agree—I am dirty and disgusting. However, what you and I sometimes fail to realize is that God sees us through the veil of Jesus' blood. God sees those in Christ as pure and holy. The Bible confirms that we are unclean; however, that is exactly why Jesus came to earth, to save us from our disgusting selves, to show us that if we had to do it on our own we would fail. So here, I give you my advice. The best way to win a war is to take away the enemy's ammunition. If you don't make bad memories, then there is nothing for him to use. If you fill your heart and mind with Jesus, it doesn't give the enemy a whole lot to work with.

For those of you who were like me and didn't wait, the Lord tells us what we are to do. First John 1:9 promises, *"If we confess our sins, He is faithful and just to forgive us our sins and to cleanse us from all unrighteousness."* Remember that the Lord forgives and cleanses us from *all* unrighteousness. I must warn you, however, this is not a license to sin. Paul shows us this in Romans 6:1–2: *"What shall we say then? Shall we continue in sin that grace may abound? Certainly not! How shall we who died to sin live any longer in it?"* We are to never think in our minds that it's okay to sin because God will forgive us later. That mind-set will bring forth a life of sin and ultimate destruction. If you are one who has waited for marriage, please continue to wait. I only wish I could have said "I waited" to my wife. Don't make the same mistake I did. My wife is an amazing person and does not look at me and think, "What a jerk! I can't believe he didn't wait for me." No, she realizes that I have sinned in the past as we all have. She looks at me through the eyes of Jesus.

Our brains are like a computer hard drive that has no delete button. Every image, every thought, every word we have ever said is stored there. It is the enemy's greatest tool.

I know this wasn't an extensive look into the mind of a male, but we still need to keep some things secret or the whole guy/girl thing could be thrown out of balance. But seriously, we need to be looking out for our brothers and sisters when it comes to purity. We need to build each other up, keep each other in prayer, and treat our brothers like brothers and our sisters like sisters. When we do this, we will be respecting them, not just looking to the opposite sex as potential mates. Above all, we need to keep Jesus first in our lives. This will solve most of the problems in this area. In the end, we really need to ask ourselves (even if it sounds cliché), "What *would* Jesus do?"

chapter eleven

Your Bridegroom

For your Maker is your husband, the L*ORD* *of hosts is His name.*

—Isaiah 54:5

It's Your Wedding Day!

Excitement and anticipation overflow you like a huge wave breaking on the ocean shore. All your planning, preparations, and patience have been focused on this exquisite day. Now it has finally arrived. Your hair is finished, your makeup perfected, and your newly polished nails compliment the gorgeous engagement ring you have been wearing for the last six months. Everyone races around the room while your bridesmaids help you slip into your pure white wedding dress. You try to remain calm and steady. You know you are ready to commit the rest of your life to your groom. You wait patiently in the middle of the room with thoughts whirling through your head and butterflies dancing in your stomach. Then, the wedding planner enters the room and calmly says, "It's time."

A few minutes later, you are led toward the entrance of the church. You hide behind the door that leads to the middle aisle of the sanctuary. Your bridesmaids begin to walk one by one down the aisle. Your heart races three times faster than the music accompanying your bridesmaids. The music fades away as your wedding party takes their places on the stage. At last, the moment you have been waiting for dreaming about arrives—the time to walk to your groom who is patiently waiting for you. You stand behind the doors that have been closed and you notice a small tear well up inside your father's eye. He winks at you and with one breath the doors open. All your guests stand to their feet, and your eyes meet your groom's. Every person around you fades away into the background, and you begin to gracefully walk toward him. Joyful tears begin to well up in your eyes while they are locked upon your groom's soft and compassionate gaze. His love for you pours out through his eyes as you walk toward him. You both can't stop smiling. You are completely ready to give yourself to him.

All of a sudden, as you are walking down the aisle, out of the corner of your eye, you see a guy stand up and call out your name. The music abruptly stops and people gasp; however, instead of ignoring him, you look toward this young man. You look back at your groom and shout, "Wait, I need to take care of this." You turn toward this other guy and make conversation with him while your groom watches in dismay. Your guests are appalled by your actions. After you are finished, you catch your breath, grab your father's arm, cue the music, and start back down the aisle toward your groom. Even still, he stares straight into your heart with compassionate and forgiving eyes. There is not even a hint of a frown or scowl on your groom's face. He loves you more than you know. But then, a different guy calls out your name and surprisingly you stop and say to your groom "Hold on, this will only take a second." You go over to this other guy. Your guests around you are astonished at your choices, but your groom still gazes into your heart with his compassionate and forgiving eyes. His love runs deeper than you could possibly imagine because he still desires to have you. No matter how many times you do this, he is always waiting patiently for you to come.

Jesus is your bridegroom standing at the altar patiently waiting for you to give your all to Him. He wants to be your everything.

This story is obviously not true and I hope that you would never do this to the guy you end up marrying. You are probably thinking about how horrible that would actually be, but here is the reality—don't miss this: we put Jesus through this same scenario often and sometimes daily. *"For your Maker is your husband, the LORD of hosts is His name"* (Isaiah 54:5). Jesus is your bridegroom standing at the altar patiently waiting for you to give your all to Him. He wants to be your everything; and every time you go out with your friends to parties and drink or smoke, you are saying to Jesus, "This will only take a second." Every time you decide to go too far with this or that guy, you are breaking His heart. He knows that your friends who don't love Him could never offer you the life He has for you. Jesus knows that a guy who simply says he loves you would never prove his love to you the way He did. *"Greater love has no one than this, than to lay down one's life for his friends"* (John 15:13). He laid down His own life so you might have life everlasting, and declared, *"I have come that they may have life, and that they may have it more abundantly"* (John 10:10). Jesus' love runs deeper and higher than you could ever imagine. Even when you stop and turn away, He still stands gazing straight into your heart with His compassionate and loving eyes. You are His precious bride, and He is waiting for you to return to Him.

Our sin nature often veils our eyes from the truth, from genuine love, and from abundant life. But Jesus is asking you to return to Him, to give your life to Him; and when you do, He will take His gentle hands and lift the veil from your face so you may see Him and know the truth, know real love, and have life. *"But whenever someone turns to the Lord, the veil is taken away"* (2 Corinthians 3:16 NLT). As a groom lifts the veil from his bride's face to behold her beauty, Jesus will lift the veil from your face so you may behold His beauty! *"So all of us who have had that veil removed can see and reflect the glory of the Lord. And the Lord—*

who is the Spirit—makes us more and more like Him as we are changed into His glorious image" (2 Corinthians 3:18 NLT).

Are you ready to commit your whole life into His everlasting arms—to the One who eternally loves you? *"The eternal God is your refuge, and underneath are the everlasting arms"* (Deuteronomy 33:27). He is knocking on the door of your heart and He is patiently waiting for you to answer. *"Behold, I stand at the door and knock. If anyone hears My voice and opens the door, I will come in to him and dine with him, and he with Me"* (Revelation 3:20). He is calling out your name. He has blessing after blessing that He longs to pour into your life. Commit your life to Him and walk down the aisle toward your Bridegroom. When temptations and distractions come your way, keep your gaze locked on His soft, tender, and compassionate eyes. Keep your focus on Jesus, your Bridegroom. Someday soon, He will bless you with an amazing husband who loves you and cherishes you the same way He does. But your focus must be on God and you must have a personal and growing relationship with Him in order to experience His blessings. There is no greater love than the unconditional love Jesus has for you. Wait for the man who desires to be like Jesus. He will long to love you with that unconditional love—the love that isn't based on looks or faults, but a pure, unconditional, everlasting love for who you are. Be patient and wait for God's timing.

If you have read this book cover to cover and have not given your life to the Lord, Dan and I want to give you one more opportunity before you close these pages. If you are sick and tired of being lonely, empty, depressed, and unfulfilled, you need Jesus to be the center of your life. You simply need to accept Him into your heart, turn from your sin, and devote your life to Him. If you feel God tugging at your heart but you think, "Oh, I have time,

I will accept Him later," know that we do not know the number of our days! Two of my friends passed away at the end of 2005 only a few weeks apart. One was twenty-two and the other was twenty-eight. One was in a car accident and the other died of an enlarged heart. Neither of my two friends had any warning signs. In a breath, they were gone. Your life could be taken in the same way at any moment. *"Indeed, the "right time" is now. Today is the day of salvation"* (2 Corinthians 6:2 NLT).

The Bible declares that there is eternal life after death: *"these will go away into everlasting punishment, but the righteous into eternal life"* (Matthew 25:46). The Bible also states, *"For all have sinned and fall short of the glory of God"* (Romans 3:23). We are all guilty of sin and we all deserve the penalty, which is death: *"For the wages of sin is death"* (Romans 6:23a). But there is hope; the rest of that verse goes on to say, *"but the gift of God is eternal life in Christ Jesus our Lord"* (Romans 6:23b).

Two thousand years ago, God, out of His unconditional and unending love for you and me, came to earth as a man and died on a cross. There on the cross, He took upon Himself all the punishment and judgment that was due to sinners. *"He was pierced for our rebellion, crushed for our sins. He was beaten so we could be whole. He was whipped so we could be healed. All of us, like sheep, have strayed away. We have left God's paths to follow our own. Yet the LORD laid on him the sins of us all"* (Isaiah 53:5–6 NLT). He rose from the grave three days later and is now graciously offering forgiveness and everlasting life to all who will acknowledge their sinfulness, turn from their sin, and put their faith in Jesus Christ as their Lord and Savior (John 3:16; 1 John 1:8–10; Acts 17:30; Romans 10:9–10). If you do that, you will be saved. *"Believe on the Lord Jesus Christ, and you will be saved"* (Acts 16:31). The Bible says, if you go on willfully sinning after receiving the knowledge of the truth, *"there will be nothing to look forward to but the terrible expectation of God's judgment and the raging fire that will consume His enemies"* (Hebrews 10:27 NLT). So, Dan and I pray that you make the best decision of your life and turn to Jesus right now! Life is too short and we don't know which breath will be our last.

If you are ready to surrender your life to God and receive eternal life, then follow these steps:

1. Acknowledge that you are a sinner.
2. Believe that Jesus Christ died on the cross for you and rose again.
3. Surrender your life to Him and turn away from your sinful life.

You can pray something like this:

> *God, I confess that I am a sinner. I realize that I need Your forgiveness. I believe that You, Jesus, paid the price for my sins on the cross. I believe that You rose again from the dead and want a relationship with me. Thank You for saving me. Come into my life. Forgive me. Be my Lord, my God. I desire to turn away from my sins and begin to follow You. Change me and empower me with Your Holy Spirit to live my life for You. Amen.*

If you have prayed this prayer from a sincere heart, you have begun a relationship with Jesus Christ, and God has forgiven you of your sins. He has washed you clean and He no longer remembers your sins. *"I will forgive their wickedness, and I will never again remember their sins"* (Hebrews 8:12 NLT).

Dan and I would love to hear from you if you prayed this prayer, or if you have any questions or comments. Please e-mail us at danandnicole@waitingfortheone.com or write to us at P. O. Box 2562, Vista, CA 92085. We pray that you will receive the blessings God has for you, and we hope you have been blessed through this book. Praise the Lord, for He is worthy to be praised!

Notes

chapter two

[1] "Purity." *Merriam-Webster. www.m-w.com.* (Accessed October 20, 2007.)

[2] Strong, James. *The New Strong's Exhaustive Concordance of the Bible.* Tennessee: Thomas Nelson Publishers, 1990.

chapter five

[3] "Fornication." *Merriam-Webster. www.m-w.com.* (Accessed October 20, 2007.)

[4] McDowell, Josh and Bill Jones. *The Teenage Q & A Book.* Dallas: Word Publishing, 1990.

[5] *No Apologies.* Videocassette. Focus on the Family.

[6] Strasburger, Victor C. "Teen Pregnancy Rates in the USA." *Cool Nurse. www.coolnurse.com/teen_pregnancy_rates.htm.* (Accessed October 20, 2007.)

[7] Courson, Jon. *Application Commentary of the New Testament.* Nashville: Thomas Nelson, 2003.

chapter seven

[8] Laurie, Greg. *I'm Going on a Diet Tomorrow.* Canada: Kerygma Publishing, 2005.

[9] Begg, Alistair. "Relationships." Truth For Life. 115CD. Ohio, 2003.

chapter eight

[10] Wiersbe, Warren. *Be Hopeful.* Wheaton: Victor Books, 1982.

[11] Halley, Henry H. *Halley's Bible Handbook.* Michigan: Zondervan, 1962.

chapter ten

[12] Sheler, Jeffery L. "Faith in America." *U.S. News and World Report* (May 6, 2002): 40–44.

About the Authors

Dan and Nicole were married in 2004 and lived in Costa Mesa, California. About nine months later, they moved to the Washington, D.C. area. There they served at Calvary Chapel D.C. Metro leading worship together. Now, they are serving at Calvary Chapel Vista in California. Dan is the high school youth pastor and also the school's Bible teacher. Dan and Nicole have such a passion for young men and women, desiring to see them grow stronger in the Lord and stand for Him in this misguided world. Dan was the twelfth-grade Bible teacher at Calvary Chapel Costa Mesa High School for three years. He also taught apologetics at the Calvary Chapel Bible College Extension Campus in Costa Mesa. Nicole has played with various worship teams for the last six years and has taught at various girl's Bible studies. Both have been actively involved with high school youth groups.

Booking Information

If you would like to inquire about having Dan and Nicole teach at your church, conference, Christian school, youth group, or retreat, please visit our Web site and click Contact Us.

waitingforthcone.com

If you have gleaned anything from reading this book, we hope and pray it would be to follow hard after Jesus. He is the only "one" any of us truly need to wait upon. If you wait upon the Lord and wait for His timing in everything, you will never lack. If you give Him your life and surrender all to Him, He will never let you down. He is and always will be faithful.

> *Wait on the* Lord*; be of good courage, and He shall strengthen your heart; wait, I say on the* Lord*!*
>
> —Psalm 27:14